GHOST PROPERTY

A REAPER WITCH MYSTERY

ELLE ADAMS

Writing a job advertisement targeting ghosts was harder than one would think.

Tonight, the Riverside Inn was quiet. Few people were in the restaurant, so my co-workers and I had decided to start on our next business venture—namely, transforming the inn into a hub of haunted ghost tours. Our first step? Recruit more ghosts. So far, all I'd done was write Ghosts Wanted across the top of a page and drawn a picture of a ghost that looked more like a blob underneath. Hey, I never said I had any artistic talent.

I showed the drawing to Carey, the daughter of the inn's owner and the teenage ghost blogger who'd got me a job here in Hawkwood Hollow in the first place. The ghost tour venture had also been her idea. She had far more entrepreneurial spirit than I did. And artistic talent, judging by her raised brows at my blob-ghost, though she was too polite to say anything aloud.

"Good start," she said. "Now we need to make our pitch."

"What are we offering the potential recruits again?" I asked her. "How do we make the idea of working for us sound appealing? Offering a salary to a spirit isn't exactly a viable option."

"Hmm." Carey's expression turned thoughtful. "There's got to be something all ghosts want. Except attention, of course."

"That part goes without saying." In my experience, ghosts wanted nothing more desperately than for the living to notice them. The allure of tourists gawking at them might be reason enough for some to apply, but recruiting the spirits was only half the battle. Getting them to behave themselves was another matter entirely. "Any thoughts on the requirements? Not everyone can see ghosts, so at a minimum, they'll need to be able to make enough noise to qualify as a haunting."

"We don't want to discourage anyone from applying," Carey pointed out. "We can stick to simple requirements at first to see how much interest we get."

"How about this: 'the job requires a keen interest in hauntings… and an enthusiasm for meeting new people.'" I paused. "If you classify 'scaring the crap out of people' as meeting them, anyway."

"Good start." She pulled out a notebook and began scribbling a list. "Right… I think we can go more in-depth on the requirements in the in-person interviews."

"True." We'd have to meet all our contenders in person, since ghosts couldn't fill out application forms, which meant I had the dubious honour of vetting every candidate. "Some can be taught on the job, if they have enough potential, but I'm not doing that for everyone."

"Good enough." She lifted her pen. "Perks of the job: an audience. Think that'll be enough?"

My brother, Mart, drifted past us, rattling the glasses on the bar.

"Help us out, Mart," I said to him. "You're the ghost here. What would inspire you to respond to a job ad?"

"Free showers," he answered.

I rolled my eyes. "I've never met another ghost who's as obsessed with showers as you are. Besides, if we did the same for everyone, we'd run our hot water bills up too high to profit from these ghost tours."

"You did ask for my opinion."

"What aside from free showers would attract you to work on a ghost tour?" I asked. "We can't pay cash, and I'm not sure ghosts would much care for benefits. Or time off."

He thought for a moment. "Entertainment."

I blinked. "What, you want me to set up a movie night for the ghosts?"

"Not a bad call." My fellow bartender, Jia, emerged from the kitchen door behind the bar. Today, the short Asian girl wore a scarf pattered with images of the TARDIS atop her work clothes. Like me, she could see and interact with ghosts, so at least I wouldn't have to handle the interviews entirely on my own. "It's cheap and easy to organise."

"There is that," I agreed. "Definitely cheaper than showers, at any rate. We can host movie nights in the games room so nobody will have to volunteer their room."

By "nobody," I meant me. I might have agreed to interview our upcoming ghosts, but I drew the line at letting them trash my room. Having one ghostly roommate was quite enough, thanks.

"Because I gave you the idea, I get to pick which movie we watch first," Mart decided.

"We both know you'll just pick *Star Wars: A New Hope* again." Some things never changed. Including my brother. He'd been dead for over eight years and still found new ways to annoy me. Possibly because he was forever stuck at age eighteen and therefore had no incentive to act like a real adult.

"A ghostly movie night every weekend?" Carey suggested. "Would that work?"

Despite the bright red goggles perched on her head, Carey was the one person here who couldn't see our ghostly companion. Her goggles enabled her to detect ghosts, in theory, but they were a work in progress, and she could only hear half our conversation as a result. When you lived in the same building as a Reaper in the most haunted town in the magical world, that kind of thing came with the territory, but as a result, Carey couldn't interact with any of our spirits. Tricky for someone who wanted to run ghost tours.

"Put that on the list of perks," I told Carey. "Mart claims that ghosts want to be entertained, which is probably true of most of them. They must get bored watching the same old sights day in and day out, and I think they'll appreciate the change of scenery when they come to the inn. Add in a few movie nights, and they'll be delighted to sign up."

"Excellent." She wrote that down. "That's it for perks. Anything else?"

"We might need to narrow down the requirements a little more," I acknowledged. "Otherwise, we'll get every ghost in town wanting to come here to watch *Star Wars*."

"And why would that be a bad thing, exactly?" Mart interjected.

"We don't want too many ghosts in here," I said. "Not more than one per hotel room."

"I didn't realise we had a ghost quota," Jia said.

"We don't, but it might get too confusing if we have half the ghosts in town wreaking havoc at the same time," Carey agreed. "The people on the tour won't know where to keep their focus if there's too much chaos around them. We want to give them a good experience."

"You'd better not kick out any of the ghosts who are already here," Mart warned. "We got here first. Also, I'm a staff member."

"We know that, Mart," I said. "Nobody is getting kicked out, but I think we need to define the criteria when we start the interview process."

The inn did have a couple of other resident ghosts, but they'd turned out to be apathetic at best at the idea of entertaining tourists, so they'd already been struck off the list of potential employees. I certainly wouldn't be kicking anyone out, mostly because trying to get a ghost to do as I wanted was as futile as negotiating with a toddler.

"See, this is why you should have kept your old Reaper textbooks," Mart said. "You'd have a built-in list of criteria."

"Mart, you built a fort out of my textbooks and then set it on fire when we were students at the academy." I shook my head at him. "Also, the criteria for classifying how dangerous a spirit is aren't the same as grading them on their ability to haunt people."

"Some of the classifications are in the regular textbooks on ghosts," Carey added. "The lowest level includes things like messing with the temperature in a room or turning lights on and off. Then the higher levels are things like slamming doors and levitating objects. That's still pretty basic for a haunting, right?"

"You try lifting things without any functioning limbs," Mart said defensively.

"You aren't going to get much more than that without straying into poltergeist territory, and we don't want one of those in here," I said. "Otherwise, skills can be individual to each ghost. We can start off by asking each ghost what they can do and then test to see if they're being honest on their applications."

"We're doing application forms? Can ghosts even lift pens?" Carey asked. An instant later, her pen leapt out of her hands and clattered to the floor, startling her.

"You've made your point, Mart," I said. "Most spirits won't be able to lift a pen, much less write their own names, but I don't expect them to. We'll do the entire application process face-to-face. Right, Jia?"

"Yep." As a couple of customers came in, she waved them over and served them drinks while I worked on adding "perks" and "requirements" sections to our job ad.

After listing the criteria, I then drew a few more cartoony ghosts, creating a banner at the top of the poster. "There we go."

Mart peered over my shoulder. "That looks like a

drawing of a birthday party. Are those supposed to be balloons?"

"It's a draft." I looked at Carey. "Someone else can do the final design. That is, someone who can hold a pencil."

"Low blow." Mart scowled. My pencil jumped out of my hand and hit me square in the nose.

"I said hold a pencil, not throw it."

Mart sent a rude gesture in my direction that made me glad that our customers couldn't see him. "You asked for my help, didn't you? So ungrateful."

"I didn't ask for a critique of my drawing abilities. I'm a Reaper, not an artist."

"You're a bartender."

"Hey, it's a respectable profession," said Jia. "I can't even draw stick people anyway, so don't ask me."

"I'll handle the design," Carey said. "I'll do it on my laptop, so we can print as many copies as we want."

"Good idea," I said. "I don't want you to take time away from your blog, though."

Carey was still working on assembling the footage of the recent trip out of town we'd taken a week or so back, when we'd gone to hunt for ghosts in another magical town called Fairy Falls. We got less footage out of that trip than we'd wanted to, and the creepy ghoul we'd found was probably too scary for Carey's subscribers, so she'd put it on the back burner while she caught up on schoolwork.

Come to think of it, we didn't need to traumatise any of our guests, either, so I added "no ghouls" at the bottom of the poster before handing it to Carey.

"It's no bother," Carey insisted. "I always planned to

advertise our ghost tours on my blog as well. Or the other way around, I guess."

Carey's ghost blog was growing slowly, though she now had some subscribers who weren't her mother or me, which was a starting point. I figured she was better off keeping the channel low-key. Not just because she didn't need to deal with the pressures of a rabid audience but because—and the same applied to our ghost tours— we needed to strike a balance between attracting enough customers to keep afloat and avoiding unwelcome attention.

Specifically, from the Reaper Council. They didn't look kindly on unofficial Reapers, and I'd already come close to accidentally landing in hot water with one of their officials. I didn't need them to show up on the doorstep and shut us down.

Carey opened her laptop on the table in front of the bar. "Do you think it's worth advertising online as well as putting posters up around town?"

I raised a brow. "Do many ghosts browse the Wizarding Web?"

"All the time," said Mart. "I do, anyway."

"That's because you like to steal my phone and laptop while I'm not looking."

And sometimes when I *was* looking as well. My brother's habit of messing with technology had got me fired and evicted on multiple occasions, since the average person didn't accept "my ghostly brother did it" as an excuse. This was the longest I'd stayed in any given location, and to be perfectly honest, it was largely because of the others' patience with his shenanigans. Such as leaving the shower running until it flooded the hotel room I now inhabited. I'd rather avoid hiring ghosts with the same sensibilities.

Granted, I'd found *this* job online when Carey had emailed me out of the blue, so maybe we could find a ghost or two that way. You never knew.

"I'll put up the ad in the same places we put up our bartender ad, for a start," said Carey, typing on her keyboard.

"Are you sure that's a good idea?" I asked. "Until Jia, our applicants left much to be desired. If it's anything like that, we'd end up with ghosts who couldn't understand the word 'haunting' or who didn't know what doors are."

Jia snorted. "If you ask me, ghosts who search for jobs online are likely to be the enterprising sort."

"I think it's worth a shot." Carey tapped more keys on her laptop. "Give me half an hour, and I'll have the poster ready to upload everywhere we can think of."

"I should have added that we wanted local applicants where possible," I said. "If they aren't local to the area, they're going to be disappointed." Most spirits were bound to a specific place, and while Hawkwood Hollow's ghostly population could move around the town at will, outsiders would have difficulty getting here.

While Carey worked on adapting my poster to a digital version, Jia and I took turns serving any customers who entered. My job was much more relaxing now that I didn't have to handle everything alone, as I had during the difficult period after Jia's predecessor was locked up for murder and we couldn't find a decent replacement. The inn hadn't exactly been a popular tourist spot to begin with, since Hawkwood Hollow's only draw was its population of ghosts, but our reputation among the locals had taken a serious hit. Between that and the unpopularity of my decision to oust the local witch coven's leader for covering up said murders, it was a miracle we'd stayed in business at all.

By the end of the evening shift, a stack of posters lay on the table, courtesy of Allie, Carey's mother, who'd helped us print them out.

"Good job." Allie surveyed the posters approvingly. "Whereabouts are you going to put these? Are there places in town where ghosts are more likely to hang out?"

"Definitely not the werewolves' corner of town," I said firmly. "Or anywhere popular with the shifters in general. Maybe the high street, but I can think of certain ex-coven members who'd just tear our posters straight down again."

"Where else is there?" asked Carey. "The academy?"

"The ghosts there might be a bit young to take on a haunting job," said Jia. "Though it's hard to put an age limit on a job when spirits are stuck at the same age forever."

"True," I said. "I think creepy children might be a draw, though they might be hard to train."

"That's a good point," said Jia. "We don't want angry ghostly five-year-olds running amok in the hallways."

"Especially as some of us have to sleep here," I added. "We'll have to have set rules and working hours for *all* the ghosts, or else they'll bug me all night."

"You're overthinking," Mart told me.

"No, I'm drawing on my years of experience in wrangling ghosts," I said pointedly. "Meaning one ghost in particular who makes all these rules look like an underestimate of what we might need."

Jia grinned. "For a start, I can put a poster up on the

door of the inn. By morning, at least a few ghosts will know about it, I guarantee. Ghosts are worse than the coven for gossiping with one another."

"You've got that right."

While Jia went to put up the first poster, I helped Carey sort the others into piles for distribution throughout town. I fixed one to the wall of the restaurant, and Jia came to help me put another on the wall in the lobby.

"I'll put one upstairs," she offered. "Where else? The games room?"

Just then, the restaurant door opened. A pale wizard with white-blond hair entered, dressed in a smart suit.

"We're closed," said Jia. "Oh, wait, never mind."

My mouth parted, then I saw Carey's puzzled expression and realised the man who'd walked in was a ghost. A fairly strong one, in fact, considering that he'd opened the door in an exact imitation of a living person.

"Can I help you?" I asked him.

"I'm here to answer your job ad," he said. "Unless I'm too late."

"You came to answer our ad?" I echoed. Not the online one Carey had just posted, surely. We hadn't even distributed any posters yet, unless you counted the ones already inside the inn.

He drew himself upright. "Yes, that's what I said."

Wow. This had to be some kind of record. "We weren't going to start doing interviews until tomorrow. Did you read about us online, or did you see one of our posters?"

"No, I saw the ad in a newspaper."

"You..." I trailed off. "I think you have the wrong place." Typical.

Jia cleared her throat. "Erm, Maura, I think he's responding to the original bartender ad. The one I applied for."

Oops. "We took that down weeks ago." Also, that ad had been for a living bartender, not a ghost, so he was a little late for that one.

"Oh," said the man. "If you're still looking for someone, then I'd be willing to help out. You can always use more bartenders, right?"

He had to be joking. "I'm sorry, but that ad was aimed at living people."

You'd think that would be a given, but apparently not.

"What do you mean, 'living people'?" He looked affronted.

"Ones who aren't dead." Talk about stating the obvious. "Deceased. Beyond the veil. Not ghosts."

He gave me a furious stare. "I am *not* a ghost."

Oh, boy. He didn't know he was dead. Well, this was awkward.

2

Jia and I exchanged baffled glances while the ghost looked indignantly at the two of us as if daring us to turn him away. It wasn't that uncommon for a ghost not to realise they were dead, but most of them didn't get to the job application stage before they realised something was off. Usually, the truth sank in when they realised nobody could see or hear them, or when they tried to open a door and found their hand passing straight through it.

This guy, though… he *had* opened the door. He'd also responded to a job ad that was several weeks old, so either he'd found an old newspaper somewhere, he'd been applying for the job back when he was alive, or he'd been led astray in some other manner. Or all three. Of all the complications that might ensue from trying to hire ghosts to work for the inn, the appearance of a spirit who didn't know he was dead hadn't even been on our radar.

"So, then," said Jia. "What's your name?"

The ghost gave her a withering look. "My name is Mr Alan Cogman. Did you think I'd let your insult slide?"

"It's not an insult," I said. "There's nothing wrong with being a ghost. We're actually looking to hire a few of them, which was why we thought you were replying to our new ad instead of the old one."

Mr Cogman gave me a hard stare. "That sounds like an insult to me. In fact, it sounds as if you're trying to deny my existence."

"That's ridiculous. I know you exist. You're just… corporeally challenged." And in denial. "Try to pick up that pencil there, and you'll see what I mean."

I pointed at the table, but he didn't move. "I will not be ridiculed."

"Think of it as a basic test before your job interview, then." I didn't know why I was wasting my time with this guy when I could just shove him into the afterlife permanently if I really wanted to, but he wasn't worth that much of an effort. Besides, I made a point of not freaking out the other ghosts in the area, which meant keeping my scariest Reaper powers quiet unless I found myself up against a particularly dangerous spirit. This dude might be extremely annoying, but he didn't strike me as dangerous. Not yet, anyway.

He reached for the pencil and picked it up. "Do I pass the interview now?"

"No need for sarcasm." I watched him drop the pencil, trying not to show my surprise at the level of control he had over his ghostly powers. That control didn't mean he was any more solid than the average spirit, though. The easiest way to prove it was by grabbing his hand, but if I did that, he'd probably walk straight back out. Despite his unappealing personality and stubborn denial of his death, part of me wondered just how he'd come to apply for a job for living people without meeting the most basic requirement.

I looked at Carey and Jia, hoping one of them would make the call so I didn't have to. Carey, however, watched the floating pencil in awe. "Wow… he really did pick the pencil up."

"Yeah." I lowered my voice. "He fits our requirements for hauntings pretty well. Too bad he doesn't know he's doing it."

"Ask if he's interested in the haunting job anyway," said Carey. "It's worth a shot, since he already wants to work here."

I had doubted asking someone this indignant about being dead to participate in a haunting would end well for any of us.

"I can hear you both, you know," Mr Cogman said. "You think you're being funny, don't you?"

"No, when I'm being funny, you'll know about it," Jia said.

"Carey can't see you," I told him. "She can't hear you either. Judge for yourself."

"She's pretending." He floated up to Carey and scowled at her, to which Carey reacted with a bemused frown.

"She isn't," I told him. "Also, just because she can't see you doesn't mean you can invade her personal space."

Carey took a step back. "He's right in front of me?"

"Yeah, but you know he can't touch you." Speaking of which, did he seriously not notice his feet weren't properly touching the ground?

"No." Carey backed up to the table with her laptop and opened it. "Give me a second to look something up."

"Ooh, who's this?" Mart interrupted, floating across the lobby to face the newcomer. "Hey, there."

"Where've you been?" I rolled my eyes at him. "Mart, meet Mr Alan Cogman. He doesn't know he's dead."

"Oh, fun." Mart floated up to him and stuck his hand straight through the man's forehead.

Mr Cogman yelped. "What are you doing?"

Mart wiggled his fingers through the back of Mr Cogman's head. "Testing a theory."

"Now you've brought your ghostly friend in here to trick me into thinking I'm dead?" Mr Cogman said. "I won't be fooled so easily."

"He's my brother, and… wait, could you see ghosts when you were still alive?" That would explain why he hadn't remarked upon the sudden abundance of ghostly figures in the streets that were invisible to most of the town's residents.

"I can see ghosts because I *am* alive, but they can't touch me because they're dead," said Mr Cogman. "Good lord, I can see why nobody else is responding to your applications."

"Excuse me?" Jia propped a hand on her hip. "*I* responded to the application. I mean, Allie called me directly, but that was because the other applicants were terrible."

"Given what I'm hearing about you and the company you keep, I'm not surprised," said Mr Cogman haughtily.

Jia arched a brow. "What are they saying about us?"

"Yeah, go on," I said. "Tell us."

I could guess, because nearly everyone related to the

coven had smeared our reputations after I'd got Mina Devlin kicked out of town. Since most of the people in question were effectively defending a murderer, then I couldn't have cared less what they thought, but I did question what had driven him to show up to apply for the job anyway.

At that moment, Allie walked into the restaurant again. "What on earth is everyone yelling about?"

"A ghost showed up," I explained. "He's here to interview for the wrong job."

"Huh?" Allie's gaze travelled around the restaurant to where Carey sat typing at her laptop without noticing the newcomer at all.

You'd think that would have convinced Mr Cogman, but he simply reddened with anger. Or he would have if he'd been alive. As a ghost, he turned more of a pale mauve instead.

"You've got all your friends in on the act, and I don't appreciate it in the slightest," he bellowed. "I'm leaving."

"Wait." I didn't *want* him to stay, but someone needed to give him a dose of reality, and it might as well be me. "I'm not lying."

In one quick stride, I shoved my hand through the back of his head, wiggled my fingers for good measure, and withdrew it.

Mr Cogman stopped mid-step. "Are *you* a ghost?"

"No, I most certainly am not." I had to admire his capacity for self-delusion if nothing else. "You're not alive. You're dead. Sorry to be the bearer of bad news."

As he kept goggling at me, Carey turned the laptop around, revealing Alan Cogman's name and picture underneath an obituary.

"Oh," he said.

"Exactly." I gave a satisfied nod. "Now we're on the same page..."

Mr Cogman turned around, walked straight through the door, and vanished from sight.

"He took that well, then," said Jia.

———

The following day, Carey took the posters with her to distribute on her way to school, and Jia and I waited for respondents while working at the restaurant. While we served customers, Mart helped by hovering by the kitchen door and signalling to us whenever a meal was ready. We'd been through a lot of negotiation with my brother to find a compromise so he would feel useful and work at the bar without getting underfoot, and we didn't need another ghost trying to act as a bartender.

Mr Cogman hadn't come back since we'd dropped the bombshell of his incorporeality on his head, but I expected him to show his face again as soon as he realised that we were probably the only living people in town who'd take him seriously. Provided he adjusted his atti-tude, of course. You'd think he'd have noticed something odd sooner, considering there were fewer residents of the town who could see ghosts than there were in the average magical community. He couldn't have been dead for that long, then.

At the end of the workday, Drew came over to the restaurant to meet me for dinner when I came off my shift. Tall and broad like most shifters, he drew some attention from the other customers but not as much as he might have elsewhere.

It might have been weird to have a date at my place of work, but the food was good, and so was the atmosphere. I also didn't have far to walk, which was a bonus when I'd been on my feet serving customers all day. Drew himself had no complaints about us picking a date spot with less risk of unexpected ghosts bombarding me with random requests, which was always a danger whenever we went to another restaurant. As the head of Hawkwood Hollow's admittedly small police department, Drew had enough demands on his attention already.

I hadn't had time to give Drew an update on the ghost tour business yet, so over our meals, I told him about yesterday's poster ventures.

"I saw your signs everywhere around town," he commented. "Carey moves fast. How's it going so far?"

"We had one applicant last night, before we even put up the signs," I said. "Unfortunately, he didn't realise he was dead."

"How can he have responded to the ad without knowing he was a ghost?"

"He claimed he was responding to the old bartender ad—the one Jia answered weeks ago." I shook my head. "Wouldn't take no for an answer until Carey showed him his obituary."

"That must have been a nasty wakeup call for him."

"You have no idea." I glanced over at the bar, where Jia had taken over from me at the end of my shift. Carey, meanwhile, was helping her mother at reception, since a batch of guests had shown up a week ago and were now all leaving at the same time. The inn's typical clientele consisted of visitors who needed a convenient place to stay while they visited other towns in the area, not people who wanted to see Hawkwood Hollow itself. We weren't exactly a tourist hub. Not yet, anyway.

Granted, we'd need some actual ghosts before we could advertise ourselves as a haunted inn, and we hadn't heard from anyone since our grumpy visitor the previous evening. Nobody had responded to the recent posters, though they'd barely been up twelve hours. I'd have to exercise some patience.

"What was his name, anyway?" asked Drew. "The ghost, that is."

"Alan Cogman."

His brows shot up. "I know that name. I saw it in our files."

"How'd he die?" If the police had known he was dead before the man himself did, then I could only assume he'd either died in an accident… or he'd been murdered.

"He wasn't listed as dead," Drew replied. "It was a missing persons report that came in about a day ago, and the department hasn't made much headway with investigating. He lived alone and didn't have any kids, from what I remember, but it makes no sense for his obituary to show up before the police were aware of his death."

"He disappeared?" I echoed. "Then who posted the obituary online?"

"That's what I'd like to know."

Weird. Maybe I should have a second conversation with our elusive ghost, but he hadn't come back since our unexpected revelation. Either he'd found some other part of town to sulk in, or he'd moved on to the true afterlife and we'd already missed our chance. I didn't see him giving in to the inevitable without a fight, though.

"I can ask Carey to check again when she's back from helping her mother at reception," I said. "She'll want to know this."

"What time did he show up at the inn?" Drew asked.

"Yesterday evening, at closing time," I said. "Walked right through the door. He's also pretty strong for a spirit, because he opened and closed the door with his own hands."

"That might explain why he was in denial," he said. "But most people wouldn't have been able to see him, would they?"

"He thought we were playing a prank on him when I said Carey and Allie couldn't see or hear him." I rolled my eyes. "Oh, and he could apparently see ghosts himself when he was alive, so he wouldn't even believe Mart. I had to literally stick my hand through Mr Cogman's face before he realised the truth."

Drew frowned. "He thought all of you were playing a practical joke on him at the same time?"

"Apparently so," I said. "He thinks a lot of himself, I'll say that much. He accused me of denying his existence and got all offended when I said half of us couldn't see him."

"If you see him again, then I'd appreciate you asking him if he has any memories of when he last knew for certain he was alive," Drew said. "It'll save my team the hassle of searching the entire town for his body."

"I will, if he'll listen," I said. "I doubt he can actually remember his death, but that's not uncommon."

Spirits often experienced a lag between their death

and their return as a ghost. A fair few of them simply carried on with their existence as if nothing had changed, only realising the truth when they encountered someone living and the penny dropped. This guy, though, had taken the experience to a whole new level.

"I figured," he said. "The department will be baffled when I tell them I need to update the file based on a ghost's testimony, but the obituary speaks for itself."

"I wonder how long he's been missing?"

"A day or two, I think," he said. "Ghosts sometimes take a few days to appear, right?"

"You're learning." I smiled at him. "Generally, no more than a couple of days, in my experience. I'll talk to him, and if he has any recollection of how he died, you can update your team and open an investigation into his death. Or whatever it is you do."

"I'll make it a priority, for one thing. And try to track down who posted that obituary."

Drew ran the town's police force single-handedly, so he had a lot of plates to juggle. This case might be worth elevating to the top of the pile for the novelty value alone, though I suspected that if I had to deal with Mr Cogman in the long term, he'd get a one-way ticket to the afterlife, free of charge from your friendly neighbourhood Reaper Witch.

"Did you say investigation?" Carey entered the restaurant again and bounded over to us. "You're looking into Mr Cogman's death?"

"His disappearance," I corrected. "Apparently, he wasn't the only person who didn't know he was dead. Can you show Drew his obituary?"

"Oh, sure." She went to fetch her laptop and brought it

to the table, where she loaded up the same website that she had the previous day. "It's in a local online paper. Pretty short too."

Drew peered at the screen. "This doesn't say much about his character. It also doesn't say who actually posted it."

That was weird. Really weird. "An anonymous obituary for a guy who didn't know he was dead and whose body hasn't been found yet anyway. Seems fishy to me."

"Yeah, it is," said Carey. "I wonder if his ghost will come back to the inn later?"

"He might, if nobody else is willing to talk to him," I said. "I never even had the chance to tell him I was a Reaper. He might have worked it out by now, though, if he's been talking to the other local spirits."

"You'd think he'd have heard when he was browsing job ads too," said Carey. "I mean, the ad didn't mention your Reaper status, but if he heard about Mina Devlin, then he'll know…"

"He'll know I was the one who got rid of her, I know," I said. "He did mention hearing unsavoury rumours about the inn, but I guess we're never going to completely shake that one. And you know, we *could* use another bartender, so Jia doesn't have to handle everything herself when we take another trip. Might be worth reviving the ad after all."

"True," said Carey. "Not a ghost, though."

"Yeah, we can start on that after we've hired enough ghosts for our tour," I said. "To avoid any more confusion."

Drew pulled out a notebook and scribbled something

down. "Carey, can you give me the website address of that obituary?"

"Oh, sure." She showed him her laptop screen while he took some notes. "Erm, sorry for interrupting your date by making you do detective work, Drew."

"No, I appreciate the help," he said. "If the ghost comes back, it's worth trying to find out what he knows."

"Agreed," I said. "If I were him, I'd want to know the truth too. Maybe we can come to an agreement."

The guy was annoying, but so many questions surrounded his story that it piqued my interest despite my best efforts. Who had reported him missing? Who had been confident enough in his death to post an obituary before anyone informed the police? And just who *was* Alan Cogman?

3

We didn't have to wait for long before Mr Cogman came back. The next morning, I was getting ready to start my shift when a familiar figure floated through the door. Floated, this time. That was a promising sign that he'd accepted his fate, at least, and I watched as he floated right over to the bar and halted in front of me.

"You're back."

"I've thought it over," he said. "I don't have to be alive to work in a restaurant."

"Seriously?" He was still fixated on working here after all that? "I thought you'd have different priorities."

He gave me a withering look. "What exactly do you think I should be concerned about?"

"The police said you were reported as a missing persons case," I said. "But someone printed your obituary online, anonymously. Don't you want to know who did it?"

"I don't know what you expect me to do about that."

"I don't expect you to *do* anything. I just thought you'd be interested. Since, you know, you're the subject of said obituary." So much for his acceptance of his fate changing his attitude.

"You're not very nice, you know," he said huffily.

"I'm positively nice by Reaper standards."

"By *what* standards?" He stared at me for a moment, eyes widening to saucers. "You're a Reaper."

"You didn't know?"

How? Even back when he didn't know he was dead, I would have thought he'd be aware that the town's only active Reaper worked here at the Riverside Inn. Granted, I didn't work *as* a Reaper, but compared to old Harold, who just sat in his cottage all day without talking to anyone, I wasn't exactly invisible to the rest of the town. My arrival had caused such a stir that he must have been living under a rock at the bottom of the river not to know.

"Until you enlightened me, I didn't know I was dead," he said sourly. "Forgive me if I'm not up to speed on everything."

Hawkwood Hollow was teeming with gossip, and you'd think he'd have heard at least one rumour, especially given the circumstances under which I'd ousted the former coven leader. He'd heard enough to know we were looking for a bartender, anyway. The details of police investigations were less widely known, since Drew took his job so seriously that he didn't even tell *me* everything unless my Reaper skills were relevant to the job. For that reason, I hadn't been entirely surprised to learn he'd already heard Mr Cogman's name or that he'd been reported missing, but nobody knew he was dead, let alone that there was a body to find. If not for that obituary.

"Do you know who would have posted your obituary, then?" I asked. "Before you were officially on record as dead?"

"I told you, I know nothing about that."

"Did you have family?" I pressed. "Or a friend, or someone who you were close to? Someone who would have known if anything happened to you?" Drew had said he had no close family members, but someone had known him well enough to post an obituary, so they must have been an acquaintance at the very least.

Then why wouldn't they let the police know he was dead?

"Why are you asking me all these questions?" he said defensively.

"Because I'm curious," I replied. "It's not every day that a ghost with as weird a history as yours walks into the inn asking for a job."

"I thought Reapers met with ghosts all the time."

"I'm not an official Reaper. As you may have guessed from the fact that I'm working at a bar."

"Then why do you object to me working here too?"

"I'm a Reaper, not dead. I can at least handle cash." What would it take to get him to drop this weird fixation of his? "Look, if I gave you five pounds and you took it to the nearest shop, then the owner would see nothing but a floating five-pound note. You wouldn't be able to buy anything with it."

"You don't have to keep rubbing it in."

"I wouldn't have to if you stopped being so obstinate." I pulled out my mobile phone. "Stay there while I call the chief of police. He has the details of your disappearance, and he's interested to know what you have to say."

"Now you're threatening to report me to the police?"

"He can't even see you, Mr Cogman." Honestly. "He's in charge of your investigation, and if we put our heads together, we might be able to figure out how you ended up like this." I gestured at his floating form.

"I don't have to agree to your terms," he said. "I came here for a job, not a murder investigation."

My brows shot up. "Murder, you say?"

"Yes, what?" he said. "I assume I was murdered. Otherwise, I'd know I was dead."

"Not necessarily," I said. "You were awfully quick to say that. You don't remember anything about your death, do you?"

"I most certainly do not," he said. "As I already told you, if I remembered anything, then there would be no need to have this conversation."

He definitely wasn't telling us everything, but until we found his body, we wouldn't be able to prove anything at all.

I called Drew's number, but the call went straight to voicemail. Assuming he was busy on a job, I left a message for him asking him to come to the inn at the end of my shift, while crossing my fingers behind my back that Mr Cogman would stick around until then.

When I mentioned this, Mr Cogman said, "At the end of your shift? You expect me to stand around and wait until then?"

"I can't go out investigating in the middle of my workday." I was doubly glad that we *hadn't* hired him, even if he hadn't been a ghost. Either way, I'd be more than happy to show him the door by the end of the week. The door to the afterlife, that is. "My shift finishes at three. Feel free to leave before then if you don't want to get any answers."

Mart floated into the restaurant through the door from the kitchen. "Oh, our friend is back."

"I am not your friend!" said the man.

"And he's in a cranky mood," added my brother. "How surprising."

"I offered to call Drew, since he's the one investigating his murder," I explained. "He got offended that I expected him to wait until I finished my shift, but Drew isn't answering his phone anyway."

"Excellent." Mart rubbed his hands together. "I've been waiting for someone to practise my singing on. I need an audience, and one who isn't biased like Maura."

Mr Cogman looked horrified. "You what?"

"You should be honoured," Mart said. "If you stay, I might even let you be part of the act."

The ghost all but fled out the front door, and I didn't really blame him. Mart's singing was an acquired taste, meaning that you either learned to tolerate it or you acquired a way of getting to the other side of the planet.

"I'm insulted." Mart turned towards me. "I thought you needed rescuing, but he seemed keen to leave, didn't he?"

"All I did was ask him to wait until Drew showed up, but I'm not sure I could have tolerated him that long without wanting to murder him. Or re-murder him, if that was how he died the first time."

"Who died?" asked Allie, who'd come in from the reception area.

"Nobody new, but our grumpy ghost just came back to reprimand me for not being fast enough to investigate his death."

"Investigate?" Carey's mother echoed. "Isn't that Drew's job?"

"Yes, it is." My phone buzzed with a reply to my message. Drew was free that afternoon, apparently, though before my shift finished. "I let him know our friend was here, but I guess he'll have to wait and question him later."

"Drew can't see him anyway, right?" she asked. "Tell you what—if Drew is free, you can have the rest of the afternoon off to do some sleuthing. It sounds like this spirit is one you want to get rid of."

She wasn't wrong. "I'll see what Drew says."

Naturally, when Drew showed up shortly after lunch, Mr Cogman was nowhere to be seen. He was probably scared that Mart would start serenading him if he came back, but my relief to see him depart was somewhat tempered by the reminder that I had a page-long list of questions I wanted to ask him.

Drew greeted me with a kiss. "Hey, Maura."

"Hey." I ignored Mart, who floated around making sick noises in the background. At least Drew couldn't hear or see my brother's ongoing antics. "I'm off for the afternoon, so I can come and help you out."

"Is Mr Cogman still here?" he asked.

"I wish I could say he is, but Mart and I scared him off," I said. "He got in a sulk when I told him I couldn't leave work in the middle of my shift to help investigate his murder."

"Did he say the word 'murder'?"

"Yeah, he thinks he was murdered, but he doesn't remember his death." Unless he was omitting information. "Also, he doesn't know who would have posted his obituary, and he refused to answer any of my other questions. I know it's not much of an update."

"No, it's a start," he said. "If not for you, I wouldn't know he was dead and not just missing. Not that it's of much comfort to him, though it doesn't sound like he'd be grateful either way."

I grinned. "At least you don't have to listen to his whining. It took seeing his own obituary to convince him he was dead, so that's the level of stubbornness we're dealing with. Might take a while for me to wrangle answers from him."

"I can be patient," he said. "I have his address, so we can always go there and see if he shows up again."

"Have you already checked his home?"

"Not in person. The team initially assigned to the investigation searched the house and found no traces of him. His neighbours didn't know what had happened to him either."

Hmm. "We'll see what they say when I tell them he's a ghost and was murdered."

"We still don't know for sure that it was murder," he said. "His guesswork isn't enough for me to make a definite call, anyway, but he might not even have died here in Hawkwood Hollow. Anyway, I thought you might want to come with me to his house."

"So I can use my Reaper senses to poke around. I like the way you think."

Drew and I left the inn and crossed the bridge over the river, which cut through the middle of Hawkwood Hollow. A couple of decades ago, the river had burst its banks and flooded, causing a tragedy that swept everyone into its path. All these years later, the water might have gone, but the ghosts remained. I saw several transparent figures drifting around, but none of them was Mr

Cogman, and none looked like they were on the way to a job interview either.

"I guess nobody has replied to our ad yet," I remarked to Drew. "The new ad, not the old one."

"Give it time. Ghosts probably aren't used to being advertised to."

"You have a point there."

Up until recently, most spirits I'd encountered had wanted my help moving on to the next world. To find a town like this, where most of the ghostly population was perfectly content to stick around in the land of the living, had been jarring, to say the least. At first, I couldn't wait to get out of town. Since old Harold the Reaper had stopped doing his job after his apprentice died, he'd let the ghosts keep on piling up, and at this point, they were permanent fixtures here. It was more trouble than it was worth to even try to send any of them to the afterlife, so we tolerated one another instead. In other words, most of them avoided me. I didn't carry a scythe around like most Reapers did, but they still didn't want to get too close. More than fine with me, but the ones I *did* attract were almost always trouble.

Drew led the way to a house on one of the side streets off the river. The whitewashed house looked well-kept, as if its owner had just popped out to the shops five minutes ago. To see what happened, I knocked on the blue-painted door.

A rattling sound came from inside the house. Oh, boy. Had the ghost got bored and decided to play at being a poltergeist instead?

Drew fished out a key from under the doormat. "My

team has already been in, but I'm pretty sure that noise wasn't one of them. Ready to go in?"

"Ready."

The key turned in the lock, and I pushed the door inward. The rattling stopped at once. I listened out, heard nothing, and then took a wary step into the hall.

The faintest thud came from one of the nearby rooms. I indicated to Drew to stay back, but he followed me anyway. I reached for the door on the right and pushed it open to reveal a living room—and someone standing in the middle of the floor.

Specifically, Mr Cogman. I took a startled step back, disarmed, but he made no response.

In fact, this time he looked as solid as a living person. That was weird.

"Uh," I said. "Hey… Mr Cogman. I thought you were dead."

Mr Cogman didn't reply. He stared at me, eyes blank, as if he didn't even recognise me.

"Sorry we broke into your house," I went on. "I'm sure you can guess why, given that I spoke to your ghost. So… what's up with that?"

He opened his mouth. A faint groan came out, but no words followed. Nothing coherent. He couldn't speak. A shiver of unease slid down my spine, followed by a rush of certainty. No wonder nobody had been able to find his body.

"Maura," Drew said. "What's wrong with him?"

"He's not alive," I said out of the corner of my mouth. "He's a zombie."

"You can't be serious."

Zombies… well, that was the popular term everyone

was familiar with. The textbook term was "drone." Or "walking corpse," which was more accurate. A dead body reanimated using magic, possessing no will of its own.

I drew in a breath. "He's not attacking us, so whoever summoned him back to this world didn't tell him to start a zombie apocalypse."

"Well, that's good news." Drew gave Mr Cogman a dubious look. "He can't see us, then?"

"Nope," I replied. "Zombies are essentially like robots programmed by their summoner. Which can't be Mr Cogman, because you can't raise your own body from the dead."

I didn't think you could, anyway, but if he'd been turned into a zombie in this very house, then the evidence would be here for us to find. The room did smell faintly of herbs, but I didn't see any pentagrams or evidence of necromancy. Not in this room, anyway.

What were you up to before your death, Mr Cogman?

Turning my back on the zombie, I returned to the hallway. "Let's see if he was revived inside the house. If he was, the person who did it might still be around."

"All right." Drew gave Mr Cogman's zombie a distrustful look. "My team didn't find anything during their search, so I'm inclined to believe he was revived elsewhere and came back alone."

"You're probably right, but the person who summoned him back from the dead must have ordered him to walk home. He has no free will of his own."

While Drew went to search upstairs, I continued down the hallway until my foot caught on an upraised piece of wood. I crouched down, and with both hands, I felt for the bump in the wooden floorboard. A piece of the carpet moved aside, shifting to reveal a hidden trapdoor.

Interesting. If the police hadn't found it in their search, then either they hadn't looked closely enough or Mr Cogman's zombie had opened the trapdoor since his return and caused it to become visible. I'd bet on the latter.

I pushed the piece of carpet aside to expose the rest of the trapdoor and reached for the handle. As I did so, Mr Cogman's hand closed around my wrist, grabbing me with strength far beyond anything a dead body ought to possess.

"Ah," I said. "You were ordered not to let anyone in here. Is that it?"

He said nothing, to no surprise, but the person who'd revived him from the dead must have told him not to let anyone through the hidden trapdoor. I fought to break his grip, but his hand remained locked around my wrist.

If I couldn't use brute force, then I'd have to de-animate him. Undoing the spell would leave me unable to trace it back to the person who'd cast it, but it'd been a long shot anyway. Zombies almost always got aggressive when you tried to find the person who'd raised them from the dead. This way was easier.

I reached up to grip his wrist with my free hand, shadows touching my fingertips. There were two ways to break someone's hold on a zombie. The first and most obvious involved destroying the body beyond anyone's ability to control it. The second was slightly trickier, but if Mr Cogman's ghost came back, he'd be glad I'd chosen that option.

The shadows from my hand swept over the zombie's

body, breaking his hold on my wrist. Reaching out a hand, I gave a firm shove, but he simply staggered back a couple of steps and remained standing there gormlessly.

"Tricky one, are you?" I muttered. "Let's try this again."

I splayed my palms and formed a shadowy shield between the zombie and me. That ought to keep him from grabbing me.

When I reached for the trapdoor, Mr Cogman walked headlong into my handmade shield. Energy rippled along the shield, the spark of life keeping him animated. I gave a firm, hard shove.

The spark went out, extinguished by the shadows. When I lowered my hands, Mr Cogman's body fell into a limp heap on the floor.

Just then, his ghost appeared behind me. Upon seeing his body, Mr Cogman screamed at the top of his lungs, and all the windows in the house flew open at once.

4

I spun around to face Mr Cogman's ghost, who hovered above his fallen body with an aghast expression on his face.

"Ah," I said. "I swear this isn't what it looks like."

"You assaulted me!" he said.

"Your zombie attacked me," I retaliated. "Be glad I left your body in one piece at all."

"You broke into my house!"

"It doesn't count as breaking in when you're dead," I pointed out. "Besides, the police have already been in here once. But we hardly expected to find your reanimated corpse wandering around."

He looked between us and his body, his expression torn between horrified and baffled. "You… reanimated me?"

"I didn't reanimate your body. I didn't even know whereabouts it was until we found it wandering around in here." Even now, the guy had his priorities completely in the wrong order, though it shouldn't have surprised me any longer. "The good news is that we can confirm that you are, in fact, dead."

Thundering footsteps on the stairs indicated Drew's return to the hallway. He looked between Mr Cogman's body and me in confusion. "What's going on?"

"Mr Cogman's ghost is back, and his zombie attacked me," I explained. "Seems whoever brought him back to life then ordered him to attack anyone who tried to get into his basement."

Drew's gaze landed on the trapdoor. "How did my team miss that?"

"It was hidden under the carpet," I explained. "I wonder what's down there?"

As I reached for the handle on the trapdoor, Mr Cogman said, "Let go of that!"

"Oh?" I gave him a questioning look. "Do you know what's down there?"

"You broke into my house!"

"Feel free to stay up here with your own corpse if you have a problem." I yanked open the trapdoor, and Mr Cogman's ghostly hand brushed my arm. His touch was clammy and cold and made me drop the handle reflexively. "Look, you're only making me more convinced you have something to hide. Do you?"

He muttered something about privacy and know-it-all Reapers, but this time he didn't stop me from opening the trapdoor. A stepladder stood in the middle of the floor below, though the darkness made it impossible to make out anything but the top rungs.

I climbed down first, surprised at how quickly my feet touched the ground in the darkness. The space was smaller than I'd expected, but I had to pull out my phone to see more than a few inches in front of me. The light shone on the walls of a small cellar, which contained shelves of… stuffed toys.

"This is your big secret, Mr Cogman?" I said incredulously. "Someone sent a zombie to guard your cuddly soft toy collection?"

Unless one of the stuffed bunnies was secretly possessed or something, then that looked to be the case. That or Mr Cogman's zombie was malfunctioning, if such a thing was possible. Since the reanimated dead couldn't comprehend more than the most basic instructions, it might be, but Mr Cogman's actual personality and life baffled me more and more every second.

Drew climbed down to join me and examined the shelves in silence for a few minutes. "Looks like they're just harmless teddy bears. Nothing nefarious in here."

"That one looks like it's plotting something." I indicated a slightly cross-eyed tiger. "I always get suspicious of anything with eyes that isn't living."

"You didn't have stuffed toys when you grew up?" asked Drew.

I grinned. "Sure. Mart and I tended to perform exorcisms on them. It was our favourite game."

"You are wrong in the head," Mr Cogman said, through the open trapdoor.

"Says the guy whose walking corpse was guarding his stuffed toy collection."

He made an indistinct noise of protest. "You've seen all there is to see, so can you please get out of my cellar and leave me in peace?"

"I only got suspicious about what was down here because your zombie attacked me when I tried to get in."

Granted, zombies had zero intelligence to speak of. If Mr Cogman's reanimated body had been ordered to keep anyone out of the cellar specifically, that would be one thing, but it might have been sent to guard the whole house and was just slow on the mark. To find out, we'd have to ask the person who'd reanimated him, and I couldn't begin to guess who *that* was.

I climbed up the ladder, emerged into the hallway, and nearly stumbled back down into the cellar when I found myself face-to-face with an unmistakeably *living* person. A man with short dark hair stood in the hallway, looking down at Mr Cogman's body, and when the stranger saw me climb back into view, he blanched.

"I didn't kill him!" he said. "I found him like this."

"Join the club." I hopped off the ladder into the hallway and called down to Drew, "We have company."

The newcomer looked even more bewildered when Drew climbed up to join me and then closed the trapdoor behind him.

"Who are you?" Drew asked.

"And what are you doing here?" I added. "Unless that was a guilty conscience talking when you said you didn't kill him?"

"I'm Mr Ellis White," he said. "I was walking past the house, and I saw Mr Cogman's door was open, so I wondered if there'd been a break-in."

"And you just happened to walk by when the police were at his house and his zombie was walking around, did you?"

"Zombie?" His eyes bulged, and he looked more closely at Mr Cogman's body. "He doesn't look like a zombie."

"I took care of it," I said. "Did you know him? Before he was dead, I mean?"

"Yes… we met once or twice," he said. "We're both freelancers who work in construction. Or worked, I should say."

"I thought he wanted to work at a bar." This situation just got weirder and weirder. "Rough year?"

"I have no idea," he said. "Like I said, I don't know him that well."

"When was the last time you saw him alive, then?" I asked.

"Let me think… five days or so ago."

"And you haven't been to his house since?" asked Drew.

"No," he said. "We didn't meet at his house, anyway. We met around town."

Then I didn't believe it was in any way coincidental that he'd chosen today to show up at Mr Cogman's house. Especially as the zombie hadn't been around when Drew's team searched the property but had appeared in the short time since. Was this Ellis White guy the one who put it there?

"I didn't do that to him," Mr White said, as if he suspected my line of thought. "I don't know who would."

That remains to be seen. "Did he mention anything odd the last time you saw one another?"

"Odd in what way?"

"Anything that might explain why he was murdered and then raised as a zombie."

"Well… no."

"That's enough!" Mr Cogman's ghost said loudly. "I didn't ask you to interrogate my acquaintances."

"You should have," I said to him. "Especially if they might be guilty of your murder."

"Excuse me?" Mr White said. "Were you talking to me?"

"You can't see him." Interesting. "His ghost, I mean. Mr Cogman might be dead, but he's still very much here."

His eyes widened. "He's a ghost?"

"Yes, and until yesterday, he didn't realise he was dead at all."

"I haven't seen him… obviously." He glanced down at Mr Cogman's body, looking spooked. "He didn't realise he was dead? Is that common?"

"That's why I want to know what happened here," I said. "The truth sank in when he saw his obituary. Do you know who would have posted it online?"

"No," he said. "He doesn't have any family, unless you count an estranged sister who's in Australia."

"Another work colleague, then? Or a friend?"

"Stop that!" Mr Cogman said. "I told you to pack it in."

Mr White, not hearing him, said, "No, I couldn't begin to guess, sorry."

"All right," said Drew. "I'd appreciate it if you came by the police station later so I could ask you some questions. I'll have my colleagues give you a call. The quicker we get to the bottom of this, the quicker Mr Cogman can be laid to rest."

"Of course," Mr White said. "It's terrible. I hope you can find answers soon."

He left the house, while Mr Cogman continued to hover near his own corpse.

"Do you think he was telling the truth?" I asked Drew

when I was sure Mr White was no longer within hearing distance.

He faced me. "I hoped you could tell *me* that."

"Reading living people is not my strong point." I was pretty sure Mr White was a wizard, but I based that on the process of elimination more than anything else. He definitely wasn't a shifter or vampire, after all. "What do you think of him?"

Drew paused before answering. "I don't think he was telling the full truth about why he was here. But it's clear he can't see Mr Cogman."

"*You* can't see me either," Mr Cogman said. "That means you don't have the right to make choices about what to do in my house."

"I beg to differ," I said to Mr Cogman. "I can act as an interpreter, if need be, but you'll have to stop being so stubborn if you want me to find out who murdered you and then turned you into a zombie."

Mr Cogman glared at me. "I never asked you to do anything. If you're going to insist upon invading my privacy and hassling my acquaintances, then I expect compensation."

"What? If anything, you should be paying us." Honestly. "We have a body here that's going to rot if someone doesn't put it in the morgue soon. Or bury it, if you'd prefer. You're lucky—most people don't get to make those choices post-mortem."

"Lucky!" he spluttered. "Must you persist in mocking me?"

"I'm not mocking you. I'm trying to be patient with you," I said. "What do you want us to do with your body?"

"Nothing!"

"So you want to rot in the hall of your own house. Got it."

"That is not what I said!" He turned on the spot and floated through the door Mr White had left open.

"He's gone?" asked Drew.

"Probably for the best," I said. "If you want my unsolicited opinion, I say you should get a team in to remove the body, composed entirely of people who can't see ghosts. Just in case he shows up and starts yelling at them."

"Good idea, but what if his body starts walking around again?"

"He shouldn't," I said. "Unless the person who reanimated him is nearby. You know what? I'll supervise as well, to be on the safe side."

"I think we should talk to his other neighbours first," said Drew. "No doubt some of them will have heard the noise, and if his zombie only came back recently, someone might have seen him return."

"Or one of them is the person who raised him from the dead." Either way, it'd be useful to pin down exactly when his zombie had returned home, or if he'd been hiding nearby all along. I still didn't know how or where he'd died, but his body didn't have any obvious marks on it. If not for the glassy-eyed stare, I wouldn't have known he was dead without checking up close.

"It wasn't one of the neighbours who reported him missing, at any rate," he said. "The report came from someone who didn't say much about their own identity, which was one reason it ended up at the bottom of the priority list."

Hmm. "If he worked in construction, why did he apply for a job at the bar? That makes zero sense."

"He didn't tell you when he asked for a job?" His brow furrowed. "I hope Mr White comes to talk to the police as I asked him to."

"He spent more time denying being dead than talking about the job itself," I said. "As for Mr White, I don't trust him either. He might not have had a hand in his death, but I don't believe it's a coincidence that he showed up here today."

"He didn't know who posted his obituary," said Drew. "I think he was telling the truth, but we'll see if the neighbours know who did."

When we left the house, I spied Mr Cogman's ghost floating next to the doorstep. He hadn't gone far, then.

He shot me a glare as I walked out. "What will it take to get rid of you?"

"We just left your house," I pointed out. "And we're going to talk to your neighbours. Or would you rather we went home and left your murder to go unsolved?"

"Fine," Mr Cogman said sourly. "If you're going to start with anyone, then pick Simon. He lives in the house on the right. If anyone would want me dead, it's him. He's probably already listening to us too."

My gaze went the neighbouring house's closed curtains. "Can he see ghosts, do you know?"

He scowled. "I haven't the faintest idea, but I don't want to see *him*. Talk to him yourselves."

"Now he doesn't mind us investigating," I muttered to Drew as we approached the house on the right. "This Simon guy might have seen his zombie return to the house without actually knowing he was looking at a zombie. If we ask the right questions, we can figure out when his reanimated body was sent home."

"Good thinking." Drew knocked on the door of the house, which opened. A balding man in his late forties or early fifties looked at us in mild confusion.

"Hello, there," said the man, who had to be Simon. "Everything all right? I heard the noise from Alan's house…"

"Did you now?" asked Drew. "Then I assume you know he's dead."

"Dead?" Simon repeated. "No, that can't be right. I saw him."

"When did you see him last, exactly?" asked Drew.

Simon blinked. "Ah, the last time I saw him was early this morning. He came back to his house and went in. I didn't hear him go out, but I wondered if he spent the night somewhere."

"Was he… solid?" I asked. "Not a ghost?"

"No, not a ghost. They're transparent, right?"

"Yes, they're transparent. You can see them, then?"

"Yes, but ghosts can't open doors, can they?"

"This one can, which is why I wanted to clarify." I didn't blame him for looking completely bemused. I was nothing if not consistently weird. "He doesn't look that transparent, either, but that's not relevant. Can you tell me what you saw?"

"This morning?" he repeated. "I didn't see much. He came home and went into his house. Ah, I saw him yesterday too. He came back late at night after being out all day."

Had that been his ghost, or his zombie? If the former, then his zombie surely hadn't been around at the time, since they hadn't run into one another. If they had, Mr Cogman would have known he was dead when he'd appeared at the inn.

"But you didn't speak to him."

"No," he said. "Wait, how did he die? Is it okay for me to ask that?"

"We don't know," I admitted. "Hence all the questions."

Simon hadn't said anything that struck me as particularly off, despite Mr Cogman's insistence that he'd been up to no good. Not compared to Mr White, anyway.

"I see." His gaze clouded. "Can I help in any way? Is there anything you need to know?"

"What was he like?" I asked. "As a neighbour?"

"Quiet," he said. "He liked to keep to himself. Never had much to say…"

"And when he did, he wasn't friendly, I'm guessing," I said. "I don't suppose you ever discussed work? I heard he worked in construction, but he was looking for a job in a bar the last I saw."

He blinked. "No… like I said, we didn't talk much. I never asked him about his job."

"Thanks for talking to us," said Drew. "If you remember anything else, then I'd be grateful if you gave me a call or dropped by the police station."

"I will." He made to turn away and then halted, spotting Mr Cogman's ghost hovering just out of his line of sight. "Oh, that *is* him."

"He can hear you," Mr Cogman snapped. "Don't think I'm not aware you're gossiping about me when I'm standing out here."

Simon gaped at him then backed into his house and closed the door behind him.

With a self-satisfied nod, Mr Cogman drifted over to us. "He's pretending not to be smug about my death. He's going to throw a celebration once he's behind closed doors, I guarantee."

"If he does, it's because you were rude for no reason," I told him. "He doesn't seem happy you're dead. He seemed kinda sad, if anything."

"It's an act," he said. "I bet he knows more than he let on."

"We can't question anyone if you scare them off," I said. "Are your other neighbours likely to know anything? Like how to raise zombies, for instance?"

He made a disdainful noise. "If I knew, I'd know who to blame."

"I don't think we're going to find the person responsible here," I told Drew. "Judging by what we've heard, I think he died elsewhere. As for why his zombie then walked home… that I don't know."

Drew's brow furrowed. "I take it turning someone into a zombie isn't a common skill?"

"Nope," I said. "Reapers can do it, sure, but few others."

"Do you think old Harold might help you this time?"

"Absolutely not," I said, "but he doesn't want zombies wandering around any more than the rest of us do, so I can drop by his house."

"Might be worth asking him," he said. "I can talk to the other neighbours myself while I wait for my team to show up. We need to get Mr Cogman's body removed and taken to the morgue, preferably before he starts walking around again."

Mr Cogman made an outraged noise. "I won't let you manhandle me."

"He's more likely to complain than anything," I told Drew. "Like I said, pick a team who can't see or hear him, and you won't have an issue."

"Do you want to stay until they show up?" he asked. "You should probably check in with Harold before it gets too late. If he knows all about zombies, then he might be able to help."

"Don't hold your breath," I said. "I'll drop by his house. Let me know when you're moving the body so I can supervise."

"Wise idea," he said. "How long do you need?"

"Most of my visits to old Harold take less than a minute." The grumpy Reaper never opened the door when I knocked, instead generally resorting to yelling at me to go away from the other side. "I'll come back once I'm done."

"Sure," said Drew. "I'll make the call. My team will be a little confused when I specify that I want people who can't see ghosts, but frankly that's less concerning than the zombie situation."

"Maybe downplay that part." My gaze fell on Mr Cogman, who hovered in front of Simon's window, staring at the drawn curtains with an unreadable expression on his face. "What are you doing?"

"He has his curtains closed during the day. Plainly, he's up to no good."

"According to whom?" I gave Mr Cogman a stern look. "Please don't haunt your neighbours. If you start a fuss, then I'll have to banish you, and then your death will never be solved."

"How dare you!" he said. "You have no respect for me at all."

"You've earned none, Mr Cogman. Dead or alive." Really, it was a pity Drew couldn't subject him to a proper interrogation. His secrets would have to wait until later, though.

Meanwhile, I intended to ask the local Reaper a few questions.

5

I walked straight from Mr Cogman's house to the town's cemetery, where a lone cottage sat apart from the gravestones. Although the Reaper had no neighbours, his house was numbered 42 for reasons I'd probably never know. Mart had decided that it meant he was secretly a fan of *The Hitchhiker's Guide to the Galaxy*, but as far as I was concerned, old Harold was possibly the last person with the answer to the question of life, the universe, and everything.

Upon reaching his house, I rapped on the cottage door.

"Go away," he said, giving his customary response.

"Lovely to see you, too, Harold," I said. "I just found a zombie wandering around. I don't suppose you know anything about that?"

"No." He scoffed. "Are you accusing me of dark magic now?"

"No, but I assumed that you'd be concerned that

someone else might be dabbling in necromancy," I said. "Zombies are our area of expertise, after all."

"There is no 'our.'"

"I meant Reapers in general." Why had I expected him to lift a finger to help, let alone a scythe? "Anyway, I dealt with it myself. Harold, has anyone in town been asking questions about zombies?"

"Yes. You."

"Very funny." Not that he'd been trying to make a joke. "Zombies don't tend to fly solo. Someone raised him from the grave, and I don't have the faintest idea who it was. His ghost doesn't either. Yeah, his ghost showed up too. It's been a weird day."

"I didn't ask for your life story," he said. "I haven't been in contact with any zombies, and I'd like to keep it that way."

"You live on top of a bunch of dead bodies," I pointed out. "Unlike me, you've actively worked as a Reaper. I'm not asking to borrow your scythe, but I'd appreciate any advice you can give me."

"You already dealt with the zombie, you said," he replied. "Otherwise, keep me out of it. I would prefer the bodies in the cemetery to stay put."

"So would I, which is why I need to find the person who did it," I said. "I could have tracked them down if I hadn't broken their hold on the zombie, but that would have meant letting it keep walking around."

"Then I'd suggest you stop talking to me and wait for the next one to show up."

"I always appreciate the help." Of course, I hadn't expected him to exert an effort unless the zombies were literally banging on his door. And even then, he'd probably expect me to handle them instead. "If the dead start rising near your house, don't say I didn't warn you."

If you asked me, it'd serve him right if Mr Cogman's ghost took up residence in his house too. The next ghost I saw, however, was my own brother, who waited outside the cemetery for me with a frown on his face.

"You visited old Harold without me?" he said. "I'm disappointed."

"I didn't know you were such a big fan of his." I glowered in Harold's general direction. "I'd have thought you'd be more disappointed to have missed the zombie action."

"You met a zombie?"

"Mr Cogman's, to be precise."

"Someone raised his corpse after he'd already come back as a ghost?"

"Apparently so," I said. "It gets weirder, though. Whoever raised him from the dead sent him back to his own house, supposedly for the purpose of guarding a cellar filled with his secret stuffed toy collection."

"His what?" Mart snorted. "I can't leave you alone for five minutes, can I? Please tell me you at least got rid of the zombie."

"Yeah, I did," I said. "I broke the spell, anyway, but I didn't find the person who cast it. Drew and his team are going to take his body to the morgue before it starts walking again."

I filled Mart in on the rest as we walked away from the cemetery and towards the road where I'd left Drew.

"So Mr Cogman is here for the long haul?" Mart asked.

"Looks that way," I said. "His body, however, is going to start decaying if we leave it there, and while Mr Cogman himself doesn't seem to mind that, the rest of us do. Drew's team will need my supervision in case his ghost kicks up a fuss or our elusive reanimator shows up to cause trouble."

"Any idea who raised him from the dead in the first place?"

"Haven't a clue." I buried my hands in my pockets as a chill breeze swept overhead. The weather in May was temperamental, but at least it wasn't raining. "I can only assume they didn't know his ghost was around. He wasn't pleased at the idea of anyone moving his body, but I told Drew to call in people who couldn't see ghosts."

"Good call," he said. "I wondered if he was going to come back to the inn, but I didn't know you and Drew went to his house."

"Where've you been, then?"

"I was doing important things," he said, drawing himself upright. "Like interviewing ghosts."

"Wait, we had an actual applicant?"

"Three," he said proudly.

"Wow, Carey's posters are doing their jobs." Finally, some good news. "What are they like?"

"Judge for yourself," he said. "Jia said you can give the final verdict on whether to hire them or not. Why do you think I came looking for you?"

"Thanks, I think," I said. "I have to check in with Drew first. He offered to question the rest of Mr Cogman's neighbours so I didn't have to listen to his ghost complaining in the background."

"Aww, he really likes you," he said. "Though I suppose it's no great sacrifice on his part."

"Not when he can't hear Mr Cogman..." I trailed off, seeing a group of police officers walk past. "I think that might be Drew's team. They're going to pick up Mr Cogman's body."

"And Cogman doesn't want them moving it?" Mart snorted. "I hope *they* can't see him."

"Same here," I said. "The problem is, I have zero idea if the person who reanimated him is still in the area waiting to do the same again."

"I hope not." He shuddered. "I don't like zombies."

"You're a ghost."

"Yes, but I have free will. They're basically creepy drones."

"I'm more concerned with who actually killed him," I said. "It was probably the same person who reanimated him, but I don't know why they sent him back to his own house. Drew and I searched the place, but we didn't find anything that indicated why someone would have killed and then zombified him."

I followed the police officers past a row of houses and onto Mr Cogman's street. The team had already caught up with Drew outside one of the neighbouring houses, where he must be explaining the situation to them. I also saw Mr Cogman's ghost hovering in the background near his own house, but nobody so much as glanced at him. Drew had taken my advice and picked out a team who couldn't see their incorporeal companion. That'd make things easier.

Drew caught my eye and smiled, while a male officer with a shifter's blond hair and muscular frame approached me. "You're Maura. I'm told you were the one who found the body?"

"No, his body found me. Well, his ghost did, anyway." This situation was weird even by my standards, and I didn't blame the officers for exchanging bewildered glances. "We found the body when we came into his house to look for clues. Apparently, whoever raised him from the dead sent him back home."

The officer blinked at me then apparently decided he didn't want to know the details. "We're going to take him to the morgue, for the time being. Is his… spirit present right now?"

"Yes." Mr Cogman's ghost moved in the corner of my eye, drifting closer to our group. "Just proceed as normal, and I'll tell you if there's anything you should be worried about."

The officers followed Drew's directions to go into the house and retrieve Mr Cogman's body. The man himself drifted over to my side, looking furious. "I can't believe you're letting them do this."

"I told you, it's the only way."

When the police officers carried his body out of the house, Mr Cogman let out a piercing scream.

I covered my ears. "Be quiet."

"They're manhandling me!" he yelled.

"Doesn't he have a mute button?" asked Mart from behind me.

"If ghosts could be muted, then I'd have tried it with you by now."

"Uncalled for." Mart sniffed. "Compared to him, I'm an angel."

"Angel of death, maybe." He had a point, though. Mart might get up to ridiculous antics, but Mr Cogman had a terrible personality as well as a penchant for trouble. And I could only assume that the person who'd reanimated his body hadn't known his ghost would come back as well. "Mr Cogman, shut up."

Mr Cogman ignored me, following the police officers up the road. "Put me down!"

It was jarring to hear his voice shouting from several feet away from his body, but his protests' only impact was to give me a headache. He didn't let up even when his neighbours began appearing from the nearby houses to watch the show. Some of *them*, I assumed, could see Mr Cogman's ghost following the officers uphill, shouting the whole time.

When they rounded the corner, Mr Cogman snapped. To my utter horror, the ghost drew back and punched one of the officers in the face. He staggered back a step, looking around in confusion.

"Mart," I whispered, "can you please restrain Mr Cogman before Drew has to explain to his officers that they got beaten up by a ghost?"

"My pleasure." Mart drifted behind Mr Cogman and grabbed his arms, to the ghost's loud displeasure.

The officers didn't make it more than a few more steps before Mr Cogman managed to wriggle loose. This time, he grabbed the arm of one of the officers carrying the body, causing them to fumble and come close to dropping him.

Drew gave me an alarmed look. "Is Mr Cogman's ghost doing that?"

"Unfortunately, yes. Mart and I will get him out of here."

I moved in behind Mr Cogman, but the crafty ghost floated out of my reach, hovering above his own corpse at such an angle that it was impossible to grab him without crashing into the officers and making them drop the body.

The ghost kicked out, his foot connecting with an officer's chin with a surprisingly solid noise. Then Mr Cogman's body fell loose from their grip and landed on the pavement.

"Get him!" I told the officers. "Quickly. I'll keep his ghost restrained."

Unfortunately, now everyone on the street could see the ruckus, and Mr Cogman had caused a huge scene without even needing to be reanimated again.

Mart flew forward and caught Mr Cogman's ghost in a headlock, while I grabbed his other arm, shuddering at the sensation of icy coldness.

"Let go of me," he bellowed.

"No." Shadow tickled my palms, and darkness spread around my feet. He stopped struggling when he spotted the shadowy outline of a door at my back and realised I'd half pulled him into the afterlife. "If you interfere with the officers again, I'll push you to the other side of that door."

He grumbled under his breath, but he stopped fighting for long enough for the officers to pick up his body again. By now, we had an audience of both living and dead, watching as the officers carried Mr Cogman onward towards the morgue. The building itself stood next door to the cemetery, so for all I knew, even Harold the Reaper was watching from the window. If so, maybe seeing the chaos would inspire him to actually help next time. I could dream.

I released Mr Cogman's ghost once the officers had safely taken his body into the morgue. He wheeled on the spot and spewed profanities at me, but I ignored him and went to stand beside Drew.

"What now?" I asked him. "Are they going to do an autopsy? Because I didn't see any signs on his body that indicated how he actually died."

"Yes, I expect they will… provided the ghost doesn't interfere again," he added. "Is Mr Cogman around?"

"Yes, and his yelling is giving me a headache. I didn't know he could actually knock his body out of their hands."

"I gathered he took you by surprise," he said. "Are you sure he isn't capable of getting into the morgue and opening the fridge they put his body in?"

Good question. "I don't think he can, but you might want to put some sage outside the door to discourage him. It repels ghosts, even ones as strong as him."

"It won't stop his zombie, though, will it?"

"Nope." So if the person who'd raised him from the dead didn't know that we'd discovered his zombie inside his house, the odds were high that the news would reach them soon. I could guarantee that anyone who'd seen the ruckus with Mr Cogman's body would spread the gossip around, but I couldn't do much about that. "I should probably head back to the inn. Jia has some new ghost employees waiting to meet me."

"Really?" said Drew. "Oh, good. Let me know how it goes."

Once the body was safely ensconced in the morgue, I parted ways with Drew, and Mart and I left Mr Cogman's furious ghost shouting into the wind.

"That guy is on another level of annoying," Mart remarked. "I almost feel like I have to up my game."

"Don't you even think about it," I said. "One of him is quite enough to deal with… and I hope we don't have to deal with him for much longer, at all."

"Me neither," he said. "Don't worry, our ghost employees aren't that unbearable."

"Excuse me?" Mr Cogman himself said from behind me.

My jaw twitched. "Why are you following me?"

"You put my body in a fridge!"

"It was that or leave you to rot in your own house—or worse, get reanimated again," I said. "If the person who brought you back tries the same again, then they'll have a lot more trouble getting at you this time. Besides, I didn't think you'd want me leaving your body to rot, either, and that was the only alternative."

He paused. "You are a disgrace to the Reapers. No wonder they kicked you out."

"They didn't. I left on my own." I kept walking. "Seriously, following me isn't going to make me change my mind. Go and bother someone else."

"No."

"What do you mean, no?"

"You had my body frozen. Besides, you're going to help me solve my murder."

"Help *you*?" I narrowed my eyes. "Sure, I'm looking into your death, but you've done nothing but hinder both me *and* the police."

Not taking the hint, he continued to tail me across the stone bridge. At the door to the inn, I turned to face him.

"Drew is still in charge of solving your murder, and luckily for you, he has a high tolerance for ghost-related nonsense," I said. "But if you do anything to annoy me again, I'm backing out of the case altogether."

"Fine," he ground out. "But I refuse to stay in my house if the police are going to keep barging in."

"You want to stay here?" I pointed through the automatic doors at the inn. "If you do, then stay out of my way. I have ghosts to interview."

Without another word, I walked into the restaurant and found Jia watching me from near the bar. "Did you bring Mr Cogman's ghost back with you?"

"He followed me," I told her. "Believe me, I'd rather not have him here after the stunt he just pulled."

"What did he do?"

"Tried to steal back his own body."

She blinked. "His body turned up?"

"As a zombie. I'll tell you the rest after I meet the new ghosts. I should get it over with before Mr Cogman's ghost starts raising a fuss again."

"I hope he doesn't, because I've already told the new ghosts they can stay here if you agree to hire them." She indicated three transparent figures waiting at the side of the bar.

After the ghost I'd dealt with today, talking to these three seemed as though it ought to be easy by comparison, though I hoped they hadn't heard too much of my confrontation with Mr Cogman.

"Hey, there," I said to the three ghosts. "Care to show me what you can do?"

The first spirit, a young man called Jonathan, specialised in making creepy shadows appear on the walls. He was followed by a middle-aged older man, Wade, who turned out to be particularly good at using light switches to communicate in Morse code. The third candidate, Vicky, looked barely ten years old. When I asked what she could do, she reached for my hand.

"This," she mumbled.

An icy grip seized my palm. "Whoa."

The girl tugged at my hand, and I bit back a wince. Seeing my discomfort, she let go. "Is that okay?"

"Yeah, I'm sold." I shook out my hand to get some sensation back into it. "You're all hired. Any questions?"

The girl raised a hand shyly, as if she were at school and I were her teacher.

"Yes?"

"What's the theme for the first movie night?" she asked. "If we're voting, I like *My Little Pony*."

Okay, that was kind of sweet. "Sure, why not."

"I've told them they can stay here at the inn as long as they're working for us," said Jia. "That way, they can entertain the guests on their own schedule as well as on official tours."

"Excellent," I said. "We're going to warn every potential future guest that they're signing up for a haunting, then? Or will we have special 'ghost-free' nights for regular guests?"

"That's up to Carey," she replied. "At least we have some ghostly entertainment now."

Three ghosts made a pretty good start to our list of employees, and the level of interest made me optimistic for the inn's future. As long as Mr Cogman didn't decide to start haunting the guests himself, that was.

Despite my threats to send him into the afterlife, I suspected that solving his murder was the only way to properly get rid of him and close the door on this case.

6

"Wow," said Jia when I'd finished filling her in on the day's misadventures. "I think you've found the most annoying ghost on the planet."

"Don't let Mart hear you say that. He already thinks he needs to step up his game."

She snorted. "I bet. Seriously, though. What did Mr Cogman plan to do with his body once he had it back?"

"I doubt he thought that far ahead," I said. "He was just being contrary for the sake of it."

"Sounds like a barrel of laughs, that one," she said. "And now he's staying at the inn?"

"Not on a permanent basis, I hope." I'd explained to Jia how our attempts to search Mr Cogman's house had brought us face-to-face with his zombie and then his ghost's unwelcome return. "I also hope the police take my advice and put some sage around the morgue to keep Mr Cogman's ghost out. If anyone is persistent enough to open the fridge and drag out his own body, it's him."

"And irrational," she added. "What would happen if he actually did have family who had specific requests for how and where he was buried? Would he fight them too?"

"I dread to think," I said. "It sounds like all he has is a sister in Australia, who probably fled there to get away from him."

I was starting to get the impression that someone didn't want me to solve Mr Cogman's murder, though the person who'd got in my way the most thoroughly was Mr Cogman himself. You'd think he'd be more annoyed at the person who'd reanimated him than with the police for moving his body, but he had the irrationality of the recently dead coupled with the strength and coherence of a powerful spirit.

"I bet it's hard to figure out who bumped him off, given his attitude," said Jia. "And now we're stuck with him."

"I made it clear that if he does anything to annoy me, he's out," I said. "Our delightful Reaper was no help whatsoever when I asked if he knew if anyone had been asking about raising zombies either. It's not a common skill, so you'd think there'd be some signs suggesting who did it."

"True," said Jia. "I wouldn't know where to start. Do you think the library has any texts on the subject?"

"Definitely not. They're illegal in pretty much every region." If anyone had access to said texts, it was the Reaper, but I doubted he'd been involved himself. He might be an unreliable grump, but of everyone in town, he was the least likely to want zombies running around on his doorstep.

"So they learned outside of a book," Jia surmised.

"From a mentor, maybe. Sounds like… well, it sounds like the coven. I bet *they* know something."

"That figures."

I'd almost rather have another chat with the Reaper than attempt to negotiate with the local witch coven. The odds that any of them would agree to see me in the first place were hardly in my favour. Jia, as a former coven member who'd quit and left town some years back, wasn't their favourite person, either, but everyone vaguely associated with the coven hated me on principle because I'd driven out their leader. According to Drew, they *still* hadn't elected a replacement, and as far as I was concerned, that signalled that at least some of them secretly desired her return. As to how it might connect to our annoying ghost and his zombie, though, I didn't know, but considering several of Mina Devlin's close associates had been dabbling in illegal magic, I wouldn't be surprised if someone had taken up necromancy too.

"I'm serious," Jia insisted. "The coven's all over this. I bet one of them has taken up summoning zombies in their free time."

"Why would they pick Mr Cogman to reanimate, though?" I asked. "He's not a coven member. They only take in witches, and even if they didn't, can you imagine them putting up with someone like him for an extended period of time?"

"Maybe he annoyed them so much that they bumped him off."

"I wouldn't blame them for that, but it doesn't make any sense that they then raised his zombie and sent it to guard his own house."

"That might not have been what he was doing there,"

she said. "We don't know what instructions they gave him."

"And we won't be able to find out without asking the person who raised him," I added. "You're right, though. He might have been ordered to stay at home and hide until he fulfilled some other task they gave him. If nobody knew he was dead, they probably figured they could get away with stashing him inside his own house to wait for further instructions."

"Yeah… but that doesn't explain how someone was able to post his obituary," said Jia. "Did you ever figure that one out?"

"Nope," I said. "It's perplexing, I'll say that much."

"If I had to guess, some anonymous person wanted it to be known that he was murdered, but they didn't call the police directly." Her brow scrunched up. "That might mean a guilty conscience, or not."

"Drew said he was reported missing by some associate of Cogman's," I said. "I'll have to check the details. Naturally, the police's first instinct was to look for the missing person in the real world, so they had no idea an obituary was floating around."

"Understandable," she said. "So… nobody saw any signs of him until he came back to life and walked home?"

"Pretty much. Drew and I spoke to his neighbours to find out if any of them saw his zombie return, but the one who saw him might have seen his ghost instead."

"Tricky," she said. "Any suspects for who bumped him off?"

"Mr Cogman thinks his neighbour is a busybody, but I didn't get that impression. This weird guy showed up while we were searching the house, though. He claimed to know Mr Cogman from work and said he just happened to be walking past when he saw the door was open."

"From work?" she echoed. "Wasn't he applying to work here at the inn?"

"Yeah, and that's another thing that makes no sense," I said. "The guy claimed he worked in construction, free-lance, which isn't remotely related to bartending. Mr Cogman himself refused to say either way."

I did need to question him further on the information I'd gleaned from my chat with Mr White, but given his uncooperative mood and the headache he'd already given me, I opted to save that for later.

"Yeah, that sounds dodgy," she said. "Maybe the guy came to check up on his zombie and didn't want to admit it."

"Yeah," I said. "Makes more sense than the coven being involved, though they might have taught him, I suppose."

"Exactly my thinking," she said. "So… which of us should go to talk to them? Want to flip a coin?"

"Or we could both go. Strength in numbers and all that." We'd ended up locked in their headquarters not so long ago, and they'd even gone as far as to use a sneaky spell to shut off my Reaper powers to hinder me. And that was when their leader *wasn't* around. The witches respon-sible for that debacle had been jailed, but the other members continued to spread unpleasant gossip and gave me dirty looks when we passed one another in the street.

"Sure," she said. "Most of their worst members are currently in jail, so that will help."

"Doesn't mean they'll talk to us, but it's worth a shot." I'd had to do some serious negotiating just to get access to their supplies to find ingredients for a spell, though I made more frequent use of my Reaper abilities than my witch ones.

"True." Jia glanced up as Allie walked into the restaurant. "Want me to ask if we can go there now? There aren't many people around, and it shouldn't take that long."

"Especially if we get rebuffed at the door." Which was depressingly likely. "I'll yell the word 'zombies' and see if it gets their attention."

"Did you say 'zombies'?" Allie veered towards us. "Is that what you and Drew found?"

"Yeah, Mr Cogman's body was missing because someone reanimated it," I told her. "Long story short, his body's in the morgue while his ghost is sulking somewhere at the inn. I can't get rid of him, and I probably won't be able to until we solve his murder."

"Oh." Her nose wrinkled. "We could always use an extra ghost, then. Jia is pretty keen on the three who signed up."

"Yeah, I think they'll do great," I said. "He, on the other hand, is possibly the most annoying spirit I've ever met, and his zombie isn't much better."

"You said he was in the morgue, though?" she asked. "Is Drew back at the office?"

"Yeah, he's updating his team," I said. "And putting sage everywhere to keep Mr Cogman's ghost away from the morgue, I hope. The person who actually raised him from the dead is still out there, though, and I have a feeling that we might need to pay the coven a visit in order to track them down. If anyone's involved in dodgy magic, it usually leads back to them."

"You aren't wrong," said Allie. "I can't say I want any

zombies involved in our ghost tours. Better to stick to the ghosts."

"Agreed." I checked the time. "Is it okay if we drop by to talk to the coven now? Before Carey gets back from school?"

"Both of us," added Jia. "I'd ask if one of us could go alone, but that might not be a wise idea. It shouldn't take more than half an hour."

"Oh, of course," said Allie. "I'd be happy to take over at the bar for a bit."

"Thanks," I said gratefully. "Have you heard any news from the coven lately?"

"No, but that doesn't mean they aren't up to anything nefarious," she replied. "Good luck."

I think we'll need it.

"I hope Mr Cogman leaves her alone while we're gone," I said to Jia as we walked towards the automatic doors. "Given what he did to the police officers, I don't trust him not to try to start trouble at the inn as well."

"Neither do I," she said. "I'd suggest putting up sage around whatever room he's in if it wouldn't offend the other ghosts as well."

"Definitely not what we need if we want to run a haunted inn."

"Ooh, where are you going?" Mart spied us through the doors and drifted out of the inn.

"To ask if anyone in the coven knows who's been summoning zombies."

"The answer is 'yes.'" Mart continued to follow us towards the bridge. "They're always involved somehow."

"They are, but it's usually hard to prove," I said. "Especially if the coven just gave advice or access to resources to the person who did it and weren't directly involved."

"What're we doing, then?" Mart asked. "Poking around for clues?"

"Maybe," Jia said. "I'm no expert, but I'm sure you need props for a spell to raise zombies, and since the herb shop was closed the last time I heard, where's the one place guaranteed to have what they need?"

"Good point." Since any witch or wizard could access the coven's stores, it wasn't guaranteed that anyone would know who'd been responsible. They might not even admit it if they did, either, so we'd definitely have to do some snooping to get to the bottom of this one.

On the other side of the bridge, we reached the witches' area of town. While most of it looked ordinary enough, the witches' headquarters was decorated with bronze carvings of griffins and unicorns, while its bricks were painted mauve and magenta. The building stood out among its neighbours and brought a tide of unpleasant memories that made me shudder.

I pushed the door inward, bracing myself to meet hostility on the other side, but nobody was in the lobby.

"Coast is clear," Mart said from my ear. "As far as I can see. I'll check to see if anyone is upstairs."

"Good call." I walked in, holding my breath, but no tripwire spells assailed me. So far, so good.

Jia followed me. "Let's see if anyone's in Her Highness's office."

The answer was no, as it turned out, and the door to Mina Devlin's office remained locked. No surprise, since nobody had taken her place, but her influence lingered on. The trouble with tracking a missing coven leader was that she was perfectly capable of using magic to disguise her identity, and that was assuming she didn't have more allies outside of Hawkwood Hollow working to keep her hidden. Drew's team was constantly on the lookout but with no luck thus far.

Jia and I went downstairs to the storeroom, where I grabbed a handful of sage in case I needed it to deal with Mr Cogman or another equally annoying ghost in the future. At least nobody had booby-trapped the door or hidden the ingredients I was looking for this time around.

I backed out of the room. "Right. Where's Mart got to?"

Footsteps came from the stairs, and a tall and rail-thin witch descended into view. She spotted us and pointed directly at me. "It's you! The Reaper Witch?"

"Really, I had no idea," I said. "Is there anyone in charge here?"

"You're not supposed to be here." She made shooing motions towards the door but didn't move any farther towards us.

I raised a brow. "That's it? Really?"

At least it was an improvement on her pulling out her wand on me, but I suppressed the urge to roll my eyes when she took a step forward and indicated the door. "Leave. Now."

"Remember the incident a few weeks ago when some of your members tried kidnapping me and locking me up?" I asked. "You still owe me for that one, and I'd rather not have to call the police on you again."

"Please, no threats." She wrung her hands. "We don't want trouble. We want you and your kind to leave us alone."

"Me and my *kind?*" I echoed. "If you mean Reapers, then Jia isn't one. But I'm guessing that isn't what you mean."

My guess was that she meant outsiders. Or trouble-makers. A fair enough assessment, but the coven's head-quarters was supposed to be open to any witch, and I technically counted as one despite my lack of a coven membership. So did Jia.

The witch cringed. "Leave. We don't want any more drama here, thanks."

"Who is 'we'?" asked Jia. "You know, you really ought to put someone competent in charge. Or just someone in general."

The witch looked affronted. "We did."

"You did?" My brows shot up. "You have a new leader? Want to tell me who it is?"

She shook her head fiercely. "No. She doesn't want visitors, especially…"

"Our sort?" I nodded to Jia. "That's reason enough to pay her a visit. As it happens, I want to ask her a question. Several, in fact."

"Then you can ask me instead," said the witch.

"Have you seen a zombie recently?"

The witch stared at me in horror. "Have I seen *what?*"

"I'll take that as a no," said Jia. "Has anyone come here and started asking questions about zombies, then?"

She shook her head violently. "You can't… we…"

"Look, just give the honest answer," I said. "It'll be easier that way."

"There was—" Her eyes turned as round as dinner plates. "Her."

I spun around. A hooded figure hovered outside the

door, peering through the glass. I barely had time to take in the figure's frightened eyes when she saw us looking and bolted, running out of sight like the hounds of the afterworld were on her tail.

In my experience, people who ran that fast usually had something to hide. "I'll be right back."

7

Jia and I emerged from the coven's headquarters in time to see the hooded figure sprinting across the road at full speed. Given the lead she had on us, we needed to slow her down a little to catch up, so I pulled out my wand and cast a freeze-frame spell. My spell missed, but Jia's landed, and the witch came to a halt with a yelp of alarm.

I hurried over to her side. "Calm down. We aren't going to hurt you, but we'd appreciate it if you don't run away again."

"Help." She struggled against the freezing spell, eyes stretched wide with panic, and her hood slipped down to reveal a pale face and a curtain of dark hair.

"The spell will wear off in a few seconds, but if you run, I'll cast another one," Jia warned her. "What's your name?"

"Abby," she whispered. "What do you want with me?"

"Is it true that you were asking the coven about zombies?" I asked.

"And spying on us?" added Jia.

"That too."

She cringed. "I didn't mean to spy on you. I was just walking up to the headquarters when I saw you outside, and when that Wendy woman pointed at me, I panicked."

By "Wendy," I assumed she referred to the wet blanket of a witch who'd tried to drive us out. "Funny, because I was asking her if anyone had mentioned zombies recently when she pointed to you. Care to explain?"

Abby shifted on her feet, an indication that the spell had worn off, but she didn't run this time. "I... I don't want to get into trouble."

"With the coven? Or the police?" It didn't necessarily matter which, though I thought her fear was genuine. "Tell me why you were asking about zombies. Did you see one?"

She closed her eyes and gave a shallow nod. "My sister."

"Your sister is a zombie?" Jia asked.

Abby flinched, her gaze dropping to her feet. "I... I went to her house to visit her, and she didn't answer when I rang the doorbell. Eventually, I got worried and used my wand to unlock the door. She was lying on the floor. I thought she was dead..."

"And then she started moving?" I guessed.

Another flinch. "She leapt at me and started attacking me, so I had to lock her in the house and run."

My mouth fell open. "Seriously?"

"It's true," she said. "I asked the coven to help me, but..."

"But they were no help, right?" Jia put in.

She shook her head. "No, they said to burn her body,

but I couldn't figure out how to do that without causing her house to catch on fire. Besides, it seems—wrong. I know she's not still alive, but she's still my sister." Her voice cracked, her eyes brimming with tears.

"I can help," I found myself saying. "I know how to get rid of a zombie. Without setting anything on fire, either."

Her shoulders slumped with relief. "I hoped you would, but I didn't want to…"

"To ask Maura directly?" Jia ventured. "Why not?"

She shook her head. "I… I've heard things."

Really, now? "Are you a coven member?"

"No…"

"But you spoke to them," Jia interjected. "Let me guess, they told you not to associate with Maura or ask for her help."

Abby gave me an apologetic look, which was explanation enough. If I had to guess, the coven had convinced her that I'd make the situation worse if I got involved. That was kind of insulting, if unsurprising, though it raised the question of whether their advice had been intended to keep me from guessing their own involvement in the zombie situation. It was just as likely that they'd advised her to stay away out of pure pettiness instead.

"Too bad for them, because I'm going to help you anyway," I said to her. "Lead the way."

Abby drew herself upright. "Thank you. I… I haven't even started to think about how she ended up like that, but I think someone must have murdered her and then turned her into a zombie."

"Did you report your sister's death to the police, then?" asked Jia.

She shook her head. "No. I wanted to deal with the body first, in case..."

"In case she attacked the police as well." Not a terrible idea, since the only way to kill a zombie without access to a Reaper was to burn it to a crisp or chop it into a million pieces. Neither option would be much fun for anyone involved.

As we walked, I belatedly remembered that I'd left Mart inside the coven's headquarters. He had zero interest in zombies, and I'd be back soon enough, so I let him have some time to snoop around the offices himself.

In the meantime, Jia and I followed Abby into a terraced street. The right house was easy to spot because the door kept rattling as if someone was trying to break it down from the inside. I could only assume that Abby had used a spell to seal it closed, but her sister beat at the door with the dogged persistence of an undead minion following orders.

"So that's our zombie." Jia turned to me. "Ah... how do you get rid of one, exactly?"

"Leave it to me," I told her. "Abby, you should stay back as well. There's no telling what'll happen when I open the door."

That depended on what instructions the zombie had been given. While Abby and Jia backed away to a safe distance away, I approached the door. With one wave of my wand, I removed the spell sealing it shut.

The door flew open, revealing a young woman who bore a striking resemblance to Abby. Her hands stopped mid-flail, and she went still, but she didn't attack. That was a good sign, I hoped.

"Hey, there." I looked into the woman's eyes. No

recognition stared back, as expected. Obviously, she was as much a zombie as Mr Cogman had been, but why had someone raised her from the grave and then sent her back to her own house? Had they stashed her in here so that nobody would realise she was dead? I doubted it, because even someone who'd never set eyes on a zombie would know there was something off about her.

I took a wary step forward and grabbed her wrist, feeling for the strands of vitality keeping the zombie standing.

In the same instant, her free hand rose and clamped over *my* wrist, leaving us awkwardly locked together.

Ah. She's been ordered to defend herself, has she?

The zombie and I struggled against one another, neither giving ground, while Abby made a horrified noise behind me. "Tara, let her go!"

"I've got this," I said through clenched teeth, tugging against the zombie's grip.

The trouble with zombies was that they tended to be equipped with a tenacity far beyond the living and no concept of restraint. When I finally broke her grip, she pushed me away so hard that I staggered back a step to catch my balance. Shadows coated my palms as I reached out again—this time with both hands—and caught the zombie by the wrist. Energy sparked against my hands, fizzling out, and the zombie flopped over sideways like a puppet with its strings cut.

Abby made a choked noise. "Tara…"

"She can't hear you," I said. "It's not her."

"I know." She sniffed again. "I can't believe someone did that to her."

Tell me about it. The young woman couldn't have been

dead for long, but I had no idea how she'd died. No visible wounds were on her body, though to be quite honest, I'd much rather leave the close examination up to the police.

"I'll call the police and have them pick her up," I said to Abby. "To make sure she isn't here if the person who raised her from death comes back."

"Thank you." Abby gave another sniff, watching her sister's body with watery eyes.

Pulling out my phone, I called Drew. He picked up right away, so I said, without preamble, "Hey there. I have another zombie here, safely dispatched. I'd appreciate it if you sent someone to pick her up?"

"Please tell me this one isn't accompanied by a ghost," Drew said.

"She isn't." At least, I hadn't seen any signs of her ghost anywhere. "But she was killed and revived as a zombie, and her freaked-out sister was the one who found her. The coven, as you can imagine, were no help whatsoever, so I had to help instead."

He groaned. "I'll send someone over."

Ten minutes later, a group of police officers showed up to take away Tara's body. Notably, they didn't include any of the officers who'd taken Mr Cogman to the morgue; despite my assertion that this zombie wasn't accompanied by an irate ghost, they probably wanted to avoid handling any dead bodies for the foreseeable future. One of the officers took a statement from Abby, while Jia and I watched from the side.

"Drew isn't coming here himself?" Jia asked.

"Nah, he's probably dealing with the officers who had to carry the last zombie and their myriad complaints," I said. "I'm not surprised none of them volunteered to come and collect this one too."

"Being attacked by the owner of the body you're carrying can't be much fun," Jia said. "Wait. Didn't we tell Allie we'd be back in half an hour at most?"

"Oops." At least an hour had passed since we'd left the inn, but I hadn't wanted to leave Abby to handle the police alone. "All right, we'll tell Abby we're leaving."

"Hope she'll be okay," Jia murmured. "She's had a rough go of it."

I hoped so too. When I approached Abby, she gave me a wavering smile. "Thanks again. I've asked for her body to be taken to the morgue rather than buried, just in case."

"Wise idea," I said. "I wouldn't ask the coven for advice in the future, especially concerning zombies or ghosts. If you want to ask me anything else, feel free to drop by the inn at any time."

"I will," she said. "I know not to ask Jennifer or Wendy for advice next time."

"Who?"

"Jennifer? She's the new coven leader."

So that's her name, is it? Jia and I exchanged glances, and I could see her mind ticking on that one.

Unsurprisingly, the first words out of Jia's mouth when we'd parted ways with Abby were, "I think we should drop by and see this Jennifer person on our way back."

"Agreed," I said. "If she's really the coven leader, then I'd like to hear how *that* came about."

She could hardly be worse than the last coven leader, but that didn't mean she'd be willing to talk to me. My shaky relationship with the coven aside, her "advice" to

Abby made her sound like the hands-off type, unless she was secretly involved with the person raising the zombies herself. Nothing the coven did would surprise me at this point.

To my annoyance, when we returned to the witches' headquarters, I found the same witch from earlier waiting downstairs. Wendy, Abby had called her. "You're back."

"No need to sound so disappointed," I said to her. "We handled the zombie. Now we'd like to meet your leader."

I expected resistance, but after a moment's hesitation, she said, "Jennifer… she did agree to talk to you, if you came back."

"Wait, she did?" Jia raised a brow. "All right, lead the way."

Wendy led the way upstairs and then indicated an office marked with the name Jennifer Ness.

"Why not let her have Mina's office?" I asked her. "If she's the leader now?"

She shook her head. "It was impossible to convince everyone in the coven to agree to vote in a new leader unless they agreed not to take Mina's old office."

Typical. At least they hadn't set up a shrine to Mina Devlin or anything, but it felt a little too much like certain coven members awaited their old leader's return. If she *did* come back, I'd see to it that she'd be occupying a jail cell, not an office, but I let it slide for now.

"Come in," a voice called from inside the office.

Bracing myself, I pushed open the door. Jia and I entered an average-sized room containing the usual assortment of bookshelves and cabinets I expected of a typical coven witch's office. The new coven leader was younger than I'd expected, with her blond hair in ringlets and her face carefully made up.

Next to her neat wooden desk, my brother floated within a lopsided circle that had been chalked onto the carpet, with herbs scattered around the edges. From the smell and the fact that Mart didn't move an inch when I entered, I'd guess the herbs mostly consisted of sage, also known as ghost repellent.

Disbelief hit me first, followed by anger. "Why is my brother trapped in here?"

"Your brother, is he?" Jennifer Ness said. "He trespassed in my office, so I thought I'd teach him a lesson."

My hands curled into fists. "He's a ghost. It's not like he *knew* you'd be in here."

"The coven has rules here that need to be enforced," she said. "I wouldn't set a good impression as temporary interim leader if I let ghosts wander around my office with permission."

"A lot of your coven members can't even see them." Jennifer evidently could, though. Had that played a part in her selection as leader? It might have, though few people would have been bold enough to offer to step into a leadership role after Mina Devlin's departure.

"It was a precaution, nothing more," she said in pleasant tones. "You may remove the sage yourself."

Suppressing the urge to roll my eyes, I reached down and began picking up the sage, stashing it in my pocket. Once there was a big enough gap in the circle, Mart shot out of the office like a rocket, right through the wall, without looking back. I didn't blame him in the slightest.

Jia, who'd been helping me pick up the sage, faced the

new coven leader. "You sure know how to make a first impression, Jennifer."

"You… you're Jia, aren't you?" She turned to me as I straightened upright. "And *you* are the Reaper Witch. I expected we'd meet sooner or later."

I raised a brow. "So did I, but you didn't need to trap my brother to get my attention."

"As I told you, he stepped out of bounds," she said. "I didn't call you here to discuss your ghostly brother, anyway. I'm told you were asking questions of my assistant downstairs."

"Yes, concerning zombies." However angry I might be with her, I wanted to keep this discussion as short as possible, so I returned to the reason I'd come here in the first place. "Seen any of those recently?"

"No, of course not," she said. "Don't you run into them all the time when you practise your necromancy?"

"What I do isn't necromancy." The term generally referred to witches or wizards who summoned the dead, but Reapers did the opposite. As she ought to know perfectly well. "Zombies are nothing like ghosts. I've seen two in the past day, though, and the most recent one was Abby's sister. She's the witch who came here asking for advice, but you sent her away."

"I know who she is," she said. "I gave her advice on how to handle the zombie herself."

"You told her to start a fire," I said. "That's not handling anything by a long shot. Also, Tara wasn't just a zombie. She was murdered. That seems worthy of a second look."

"I assumed Abby intended to report the incident to the police," she said.

She had, but Jennifer's reluctance to get involved still drew my suspicions.

"She's the second zombie I've seen today, so it would have helped if someone had told me sooner," I said. "Abby seemed to be under the impression that speaking to me would land her in trouble with the coven. I wonder what would give her that idea?"

"I certainly never said such a thing,' said Jennifer. "Did you say, 'second zombie'? What did you do with the first?"

Now, why would she want to know that? "The first was murdered, too, except the police had him listed as missing and not dead. I took care of him, same as Abby's sister."

"How interesting." She looked at me for a moment as if assessing me. "The truth of the matter is that Tara wasn't the only person who disappeared this week. A member of the coven did too."

"Someone else disappeared?" asked Jia.

"Yes," said Jennifer. "Given the timing, I have cause to be concerned."

"I bet." Was her worry an act, or did the incident genuinely take her off guard? It wasn't that much of a reach for her to have brushed off Abby's woes because Abby wasn't a coven member but then changed her tune when one of her own witches went missing. That was pure speculation on my part, though. "Have you called the police yet?"

"I believe this needs more than the police's involvement," she said. "It needs a Reaper."

8

"So the coven decided to take the law into their own hands?" Drew asked me across the cluttered desk of his office at the police station. I'd gone there directly to explain Jennifer's offer in person rather than over the phone, ignoring the disgruntled looks the other officers shot at me. "Including not reporting missing members to the police?"

"Seems that way," I replied. "I barely convinced her to let me come here and talk to you first."

Meanwhile, Jia had offered to return to the restaurant and explain my whereabouts to Allie on the condition that I immediately told her everything upon my return. One of us had to go back to work after all, but we might have limited time to find the missing coven member before she turned into a zombie too. Assuming we weren't already too late to spare her that fate.

"They've also been warning non-members to avoid contacting me," I added. "Which has now come back to bite them in a major way."

"You said yes, though?"

"Didn't have much choice." I never thought I'd ever *help* the coven, but I had a marked absence of any other options. If their missing coven member turned out to be both dead and reanimated like Abby's sister had been, then I was the only person who could get rid of her. Zombies aside, three deaths under similar circumstances would normally imply a serial killer was on the loose in town.

A serial killer who raised their victims from the dead after the fact. That was a new one for me, and I expected the same was true of the police. Even in the magical world.

"Who is this new coven leader, then?" Drew asked me as we left the police station. "I haven't met her, which is a strike against her, considering I seem to remember the coven promising to notify the police when they appointed someone new as their leader."

"She'll be thrilled when you show up at her office, then," I said. "They couldn't have expected to get away with avoiding you, but she's the sort who prefers to stay out of the action unless it concerns the coven directly. Oh, and unless you count my brother's ghost wandering into her office. She trapped him in a circle of sage just to prove a point."

"Another strike against her, then." His expression darkened. "I've had my hands full with the werewolf pack, so I haven't been as vigilant with watching the coven as I should have been."

"It's more her fault than yours," I said. "It sounds like the coven only voted her into her position if she made it clear she wouldn't be taking Mina's place. Even her old office is out of bounds."

"Definitely fishy," Drew said. "That said, I'll reserve judgement on this Jennifer Ness until I can meet her myself."

"All right." I held up my phone, into which I'd typed the name and address Jennifer had given me. "This coven member, Marilyn, supposedly lives alone. We're not far from her house, I think."

As we rounded a corner, Drew leaned over to check the address on my phone screen. "I wonder if anyone's actually been there to check on her? I find it hard to believe that they've concluded that she's missing without visiting her house at the very least."

"Jennifer hasn't been there herself, but like I said, she favours a hands-off approach," I replied. "If I had to guess, the person who reported her missing did look around her house. Whether she told the truth or not remains to be seen."

"Precisely my thinking."

"Though if it turns out that she *is* a zombie, then I don't know that I can fault the witch who found her for not calling the police. Abby didn't."

"She told Jennifer, though."

Whatever the case, the new coven leader had clearly been reluctant to ask for the aid of the person who'd ousted their former leader. Her behaviour suggested she'd exhausted all other possible options. Unless this was all a trap, of course.

Having already seen two zombies today, I already pretty much expected this third visit to end in the same way whether it was a trap or not, so I strode into the lead when we found the right street. Marilyn's house didn't look sealed with magic, nor did the door tremble in its frame as if a zombie were trying to break it down the way Abby's sister had. Regardless, I stood back as I cast an unlocking spell on the door, which sprang open.

Nobody waited on the other side, zombie or otherwise. The narrow hallway smelled a bit musty but more of neglect than decay. By mutual agreement, Drew searched upstairs while I explored the downstairs floor, peering into each room. Nothing stood out as suspicious to me at all.

Drew returned to the hallway. "She's not here."

"I'll check for her ghost." I called the shadows to my hands and peered into the afterworld. "Marilyn?"

No response came. That didn't mean she was alive, of course, thanks to the common delay between a person's death and the appearance of their ghost. Yet the absence of her zombie surprised me more than her ghost's silence. Why had Jennifer thought there might be a connection with Abby's sister?

"Maybe she was murdered elsewhere... or she's still alive," I suggested. "Where was she last seen, I wonder?"

"We'll speak to the coven leader and see what she says," he said. "If we let her know that there's a chance that Marilyn might be alive, then she might be willing to cooperate with us."

"We can dream," I said. "It's not a good sign that she appointed herself the leader without asking you, when you were supposed to supervise the process."

"True, but I can't complain about being left out when I had enough trouble handling the werewolves when they picked *their* new leader."

"I bet." The furore that had erupted a few weeks ago when the werewolves' former leader retired was also one of the reasons he hadn't been able to come with Carey and me on our ghost-hunting trip to Fairy Falls. Being head of the police kept him busy enough already, but it would have been nice to have a little time away together before the madness began again.

At least Jennifer Ness would have to introduce herself to the police now her coven genuinely needed their help, but I couldn't figure out whether my misgivings about her came from her predecessor or her own actions. What she'd done to Mart was proof enough that she wasn't to be trusted. I could only assume he was hiding back at the inn, but I'd have to talk to him later.

Meanwhile, Drew and I returned to the witches' headquarters, where we went straight up to Jennifer's office. Wendy assailed us at the door and followed us upstairs, wringing her hands, which we both ignored.

When we entered the new coven leader's office, Jennifer didn't appear to have moved an inch from her position behind her desk, and she didn't appear surprised to see the head of the police force walk in either.

She surveyed us with a calm expression. "You're Drew Gardener, are you?"

"I am," said Drew. "I believe the coven and I came to a mutual agreement that the next leader they voted in would introduce themselves to me before taking the position."

Jennifer's unflappable countenance remained in place. "I understand, but I'm not the coven leader in an official sense. I'm simply the person the coven has chosen to steer them through the interim period between leaders."

Isn't that the same thing? I bit back the comment as we had more important subjects to discuss, though if you asked me, the coven was hopeless at policing itself no matter who was in charge.

"We'll discuss the matter later," said Drew, seemingly agreeing to let the subject drop for now. "Firstly, I'd like to talk to you about your missing coven member."

"Found her, did you?"

"No," he replied. "Her house was deserted, in fact, which suggests that she might still be alive. If so, then to find her, I'll need your cooperation. I would like you to give me the details of when she was last seen and by whom."

"How deductive of you," she said. "In answer to your request, Marilyn was last seen leaving her house yesterday afternoon."

"Who reported her as missing?"

"Another coven member who was going to attend a meeting with her."

They were holding coven meetings again, were they? That was either a sign that Jennifer had truly taken the wheel, or an indication that they were up to their old tricks again. I didn't need to worry about the coven's shenanigans when we had a killer to catch, though— unless, of course, the coven was responsible.

"Was this the first time a disappearance within the coven was reported to you?" Drew asked.

"Yes, it was."

"Except Tara's, though she's not in the coven," I put in. "Any *non*-coven disappearances you're aware of?"

"If there were, I'd have told you earlier."

Right. As if I'm not a last resort. Though given what I'd seen so far, the odds that she was being honest were higher than I'd initially expected.

"Are there any other suspicious events you'd like me to know about?" Drew asked. "From within your coven or otherwise?"

"Are you asking me to do your job for you?"

"Certainly not," he said, with far more patience than I'd have shown in his place. "I simply wondered if there were more illicit activities that were not reported to the police. Aside from the fact that I was not informed of your new leadership, I'm also hearing stories that your coven is warning members and non-members alike against sharing information with outsiders. Particularly with Maura, which seems counterproductive at a time like this."

"A time like this?" she echoed. "Care to elaborate on that?"

Drew wore a grave expression. "We have a murderer on the loose who also happens to be dabbling in dangerous magic. Now, in my experience, magic is more commonly learned from a coven than anywhere else. Yes, it might be the work of an individual or a select group without the coven's knowledge, but if you're aware of any resources from which the culprit might have learned how to cast the spell they used on the bodies they reanimated, then I'd appreciate it if you let me know."

"I'm aware that this is a matter of great concern for you," she said. "But I know nothing of necromancy, nor do I see any reason to believe anyone in my coven has been sharing this knowledge. It looks more like the work of a lone fanatic."

"The circumstances of the first victim's death were

suspicious enough to make me certain that the person doing this intended to draw attention," Drew said. "He was initially reported missing, not dead, though in his case, the police were contacted first. If anyone else goes missing, then I'd be grateful if you let me know right away."

"How interesting," she said. "I know nothing that I haven't already told you, but if that changes, I'll be sure to send the details to you."

"I'll hold you to that," Drew replied.

I watched Jennifer's face carefully, trying to discern if she knew any more than she let on. It was hard to let go of my own paranoia about the ex-coven leader, but would this woman really cover up for a serial killer who'd murdered people in some undisclosed place and then brought them back as zombies? I didn't know her well enough to make a definite judgement call.

"I'll talk to you both again soon." Jennifer's tone contained a clear note of dismissal, which was more than fine with me.

"I expect we'll have another discussion soon," Drew agreed. "I hope Marilyn is found safely."

On that note, we left the office and headed downstairs, once again ignoring Wendy's incessant hovering. She tailed us all the way to the door, as if she expected us to turn around and try to kidnap her beloved leader or something. If she were my assistant, I'd have fired her within the first hour.

"Well, that was instructive," I said to Drew when the door closed behind us. "She didn't seem entirely sincere. I don't see her falling over herself to call the police as soon as she has news and not as a last resort."

"Then I'll have to call her instead," he said. "For the record, I don't think she's the one doing this."

"No, but she might be covering for someone who did. Even Mina Devlin wasn't the one wielding the weapon." Most of her crimes had involved burying other people's evil deeds instead. "I was ninety percent sure she was leading us into a trap when she gave us the address."

"The thought crossed my mind too," Drew said. "Where're you off to next?"

"I should go back to work, but first I thought I might try to find Marilyn's ghost again—or Tara's."

I might need to wait a bit longer for Marilyn, but Tara's ghost had had ample time to return without necessarily moving on to the next world. If the living wouldn't talk, then I'd have to ask the dead instead.

Drew insisted on accompanying me to the morgue, where I noticed that someone had taken my advice and sprinkled a line of sage by the door. Only time would tell if that would be enough to keep Mr Cogman out, but I didn't see any signs of him.

Opting to stay outside, I called the shadows to my hands and opened the afterworld at such an angle that Drew would be able to see and hear everything I did.

Shadows flooded my palms, and I faced the afterworld. "Tara?"

I didn't expect an answer, so I jumped back a step when Tara herself appeared in the dark mass in front of me. Identical to her zombie self except for an added hint of transparency, she released a piercing scream.

"Whoa," I said. "Calm down. I'm not here to harm you. I met your sister."

"You're the Reaper." Tara spun around, staring at the

shadows cloaking both of us. "Where did you meet my sister?"

"I'm afraid she's the one who found your body."

"So I'm really gone." She stopped spinning, her gaze fixating on me. "I'm dead."

"You are," I said, keeping my voice soft. "It also appears that you were murdered, and you might not be the only victim. Do you remember anything about how you died?"

She shook her head. "No. I remember being somewhere dark when I woke up like this, but I... I don't remember how I got there."

"Was your body nearby?"

"I didn't see," she murmured. "It was so dark in there, and it took me ages to find my way out."

"So you weren't killed at your house?"

"No... why?"

"That was where your sister found you."

"What?" She stared at me in horror. "She found me at home?"

"Yes, she did." *Wait. She doesn't know.* "Did you know the killer raised you from the dead as a zombie?"

She recoiled. "What?"

Oh boy. If she'd been in the dazed-and-confused post-death state most spirits experienced, then she might not have realised what was happening to her body.

"You were revived as a zombie," I repeated. "And sent back to your house. I don't know who did it, but when your sister found you, your zombie tried to attack her."

"What?" Her voice turned shrill. "No, no, no! Is she okay?"

"She's fine," I said. "I safely removed the spell controlling your body, but do you remember who did it to you?"

"No." A pause. "I remember it being dark—before too. I think I was blindfolded."

That would explain why she didn't recall anything of her surroundings. A killer with enough knowledge to raise her as a zombie would have anticipated their ghosts' potential return as well, so they'd evidently picked a dark enough location that the victims' ghosts wouldn't be able to remember their deaths. "Were there any other ghosts around?"

"No." Her voice was quiet. "I was the only one."

Strange. Really strange. "Did you manage to find your way outside? Or were you still in the dark place when I called you here?"

"No... I escaped last night, I think. It's all a blur, but... but I remember being in a field the first time I was able to see my surroundings."

"Near Hawkwood Hollow?" It must have been if she had found her way back here. "Do you think you'd be able to find the place again in daylight?"

"I don't know. Probably not. Like I said, it was dark..."

"Then why'd your murderer send your zombie back home?" That part, I was still lost on, in addition to why the killer had raised their victims from the dead in the first place.

"I don't know," Tara said quietly. "I don't know."

"Thanks for the help." I let the shadows drop and turned to Drew. He'd watched silently throughout our conversation, wearing a grim expression.

"If she's right, then the killer has some kind of hideout outside of the town itself," he said. "Potentially with more victims locked up in there."

"Yeah. It's sick." In fact, whether Marilyn survived or

not, she might still be in the killer's lair right this instant. "I couldn't find Marilyn's ghost, so I can't track her yet."

Unfortunately, my ability to track an individual was severed upon their death. I could track ghosts but not dead bodies, reanimated or otherwise.

"It'll be dark soon," Drew added. "Searching the fields around town at night will take forever, and if I mention to my officers that there might be other zombies around, I can guarantee I won't get any volunteers to go out there."

I groaned. "Meaning it's up to us. Unless you can think of anyone who might know if there are any abandoned old buildings out in the fields around Hawkwood Hollow."

"I'll talk to the police department of the neighbouring town," said Drew. "Let them know there's a killer on the loose in the area. They might be targeting people from there too."

"You want to ask if the normals have recently had a swarm of zombies?"

"I won't mention that part," he said. "Pity the ghost couldn't give you directions."

"No… but someone else might."

If the victims were all killed in the same place, then Mr Cogman must have been among them. Time for another chat with the most annoying ghost on the planet.

9

The first thing I did upon getting back to the inn was scan the restaurant for Mr Cogman's ghost. Jia waved at me from behind the bar, while Carey sat at a nearby table, doing her homework, but no ghosts materialised.

"Hey." Carey brightened when she saw me walk over. "I wondered where you'd got to."

"I've had a day of it." I joined Jia at the bar. "I don't suppose you've seen our favourite ghost?"

"Me?" Mart popped up before Jia could answer.

"No, our new friend."

"You want to find *him?*" said Mart.

"I don't have much choice." I drew in a breath. "It turns out we have a serial killer who's murdering people in some unknown location and then sending their zombies back home. If the missing coven member is still alive, then she must be in the same place."

Jia's jaw dropped. "You mean she's in the serial killer's lair?"

"I would guess so, but Tara's ghost doesn't remember the way," I explained. "Mr Cogman, however, seems like the sort of guy who keeps track of the details."

She snorted. "He probably complained loudly the entire time he was being murdered too."

Carey lifted her head. "Wait, who got murdered this time?"

"I told Carey everything," Jia added, for my benefit. "Except whatever you just found out. Did you really talk to Tara's ghost?"

"Yeah, she's pretty shaken up," I said. "She claimed she was blindfolded and then killed in somewhere too dark to see even as a ghost. When she got outside, she found herself in a field, so our elusive killer must be hiding somewhere outside of Hawkwood Hollow."

"That's why you need directions," Jia surmised. "From Mr Cogman."

"Wherever he is." Typical of him to disappear the one time I actually needed to find him. It was already getting late, and I didn't have the patience to search every room in the entire inn, so I'd need to use a shortcut. "I hope that if I tell him someone's life hangs in the balance, he might cooperate for once."

He hadn't been in the best of moods the last time we'd seen one another, but what choice did I have? Marilyn's life might depend on me getting through to him.

I let shadows cover my hands, and the afterworld unfolded around me. "Mr Cogman? Are you there?"

"What?" He appeared before me, an indignant expression on his ghostly face. "How dare you summon me as if I were a mere servant? You have no respect."

"I have no time," I corrected. "I want you to take me to the place where you were murdered."

"And why should I do that?"

"Because the serial killer has captured another victim, and saving her life might depend on us finding where they're keeping her."

"Serial killer?" he scoffed. "What serial killer?"

"The one who murdered you," I said. "And Tara too. We know they're based in a lair in the fields surrounding Hawkwood Hollow, but we need someone who's been there to give us directions."

"What are you talking about?" he said. "I was murdered on a street on the outskirts of town. Someone ambushed me from behind and struck me over the head."

"You…" I trailed off. "You might have told me that earlier."

"You never asked."

"I'm trying to solve your murder. I thought you didn't remember anything about your death." I couldn't believe he'd omitted such a major piece of information. "Were you ever planning to tell me? Or did you want to watch me stumble around forever?"

"Tell you what?" Carey asked from behind me, unable to restrain her curiosity for a moment longer. "Does he remember his death?"

"Yes, but he wasn't killed in the same way as the others," I said. "Or in the same place, either. I need to tell Drew."

"You most certainly will not," he said. "How and where a man dies is his own business."

"You," I said, "are the most ridiculous ghost I've ever met."

"I'm taking that as a challenge," Mart said from somewhere nearby. "Just so you know."

"I have had enough of being disrespected!" Mr Cogman bellowed. "You have the nerve to drag me here to ask intrusive questions—"

"You invited yourself to stay at the inn until we solved your murder," I pointed out. "Now it turns out you've been holding out on us. If you ever skip out on sharing important information from me again, then you'll get a one-way ticket to the afterlife. Immediately."

He gaped at me. "That won't be necessary. I'd have told you if you asked me."

"A likely story." My hands itched to shove him into the permanent afterlife to avoid any future grief from him, but instead I grabbed my phone and called Drew.

"Maura?" He sounded slightly breathless, as if he was speaking into the phone while doing something else.

"Hey. There's a slight issue. Mr Cogman wasn't murdered in the same location as the others, which he's neglected to tell me until now."

"Oh." A pause followed, in which I could hear discordant shouts and shuffling noises. "I'm sorry, but there's no need to bring him along to help look for Marilyn anyway."

My heart sank. "Why?"

"Because my team is currently wrangling her zombie right this instant. She turned up herself, shambling down the high street."

I groaned. "I'll be right over."

———

One dispatched zombie later, I stood outside the morgue yet again, watching the officers carry Marilyn's body inside. I'd dealt with her zombie in the same way as the others, and she hadn't put up too much of a fight, but I still felt I'd let her down by not finding her sooner.

I released a sigh. "So, which of us is going to break the bad news to Jennifer Ness?"

"I will," Drew said. "This is going to make things difficult with the coven, I expect, but she won't be able to deny that we're looking at the work of a dangerous magical killer."

"Assuming she isn't part of it herself." Regardless, Mr Cogman's revelation had thrown a wrench in our attempts to find a clue leading to the killer's location. "I'll see if Marilyn's ghost shows up and sheds some light on whereabouts she was killed. Though if she was wandering the street as a zombie, you'd think someone would have spotted her before she reached the high street."

"It's hard to tell a zombie from a regular person unless you see them close up," he said. "That's what has my officers so rattled. I expect I'll be dealing with excuses and false alarms for the foreseeable future, or at least until this case is dealt with."

"Fun." I looked up at the darkening sky. "I need to head back to the inn. I can try to wrangle some more answers from Mr Cogman."

"He claims someone hit him on the head from behind, did he?" Drew said. "The autopsy will be able to back up his claim, or otherwise."

"When's that?"

"It's scheduled for tomorrow," he said. "Marilyn and

Tara will be examined, too, since their bodies had no marks on them."

"That suggests they were both killed with magic." Not Mr Cogman, though. The serial killer had broken the pattern with him, which implied he had no connection with the other murders at all—if he hadn't also been turned into a zombie.

After parting ways with Drew, I walked back to the inn in a foul mood that only intensified when I found no signs of Mr Cogman's spirit inside the restaurant. Our new ghostly employees all backed away when they saw me, so I attempted to tamp down my anger. Despite their fellow ghost's behaviour, they hadn't done anything wrong.

"Hey," I said to them. "Have you seen Mr Cogman?"

"He went that way." Jonathan pointed hesitantly through the doorway. "Is he going to stay here?"

"Until I find his killer," I said. "Sorry if I freaked you out earlier. I thought he had information on a serial killer I'm searching for, and I was counting on his cooperation. You might have noticed he doesn't have much of that going spare."

"I'll keep an eye out for him," the ghost promised.

"Cheers." I left their group and approached the bar, where Jia was chatting with Carey.

"Another zombie?" asked Carey.

"Yeah." I slumped into a seat. "We were too late to save her, but we'd never have got to the killer's hideout in time anyway."

"Why turn them into zombies and send them back into town?" Jia asked. "That's what I don't get."

"Believe me, I've been wondering the same thing."

"Did you find her ghost, though?" asked Carey.

"Not as yet, but I'll keep trying," I said. "There's often a delay, but Tara's ghost did show up. Maybe Marilyn's will too."

That didn't mean she'd be able to point me in the right direction. Tara had been kidnapped, blindfolded, and taken to an undisclosed location and then murdered and revived as a zombie, none of which she'd actually seen with her own eyes. If her testimony was accurate, then she'd been in total darkness until her escape.

If Marilyn's own memories turned out to be equally unreliable, then we'd need to find some other way to track down the killer's location. preferably before they claimed another victim.

————

I paid another visit to the coven the following day. I hadn't intended to—that was supposed to be Drew's job—but he was visiting the police office in the neighbouring town to warn them a serial killer was running loose in the area. How he'd get through that conversation without accidentally mentioning magic was beyond me. I'd had enough trouble avoiding mentioning ghosts when I'd lived among normals myself, but a magical serial killer was on another level entirely.

I walked over the bridge alone after my lunch break, as Jia and I had agreed to trade shifts so that she had the morning off and I had the afternoon free to meet up with Jennifer Ness. Mart had declined to come with me, which might have had more to do with the zombies than the coven leader's tendency to trap unsuspecting ghosts in her office if they strayed out of bounds. Instead, I'd sent him to keep an eye on Mr Cogman, who'd been avoiding me since our confrontation yesterday.

Not entirely a surprise, given that when I'd threatened to send him to the afterlife, I'd meant every word. If he didn't have any valuable information to share with me, then I'd dispose of him the next time he crossed a line and wash my hands of the whole matter.

After entering the lobby of the witches' headquarters, I climbed the stairs and knocked on the door to Jennifer Ness's "office." I expected to find the leader in a foul mood, since her coven member had turned up dead and zombified, but when I entered, she looked across her desk at me with her expression as impassive as ever.

"I'm sorry for your loss," I began.

"No, you aren't."

"I am." I closed the door behind me and approached her desk. "Marilyn didn't deserve to die any more than Tara did. I wish we'd managed to find her beforehand, and so do the police."

"The police's lofty promises amounted to nothing."

"She was already dead long before you contacted the police, Jennifer," I said. "Just be glad we caught her reanimated body before the person responsible could hide their crime."

"I'll be glad when her murderer is brought to justice," she said. "The head of the police paid me a brief visit earlier, and what he told me didn't fill me with confidence that he knew how to handle this."

"Drew is currently talking to the police department of

the neighbouring town," I told her. "Finding the killer's hideout will require searching an extensive area outside of Hawkwood Hollow." Unless one of the victims' ghosts could give us a shortcut, of course.

"He's talking to the normals?" Scepticism layered her tone.

"Yes, to find out if there have been any other victims." Reanimating someone as a zombie in a non-magical town was a crime on several other levels than in a magical community, not least because zombies tended to draw the kind of attention that might clue people in to an unseen magical world beneath their own. That couldn't be the killer's end goal, though, because there were far easier ways to expose our world that didn't involve serial murder and reanimating corpses. "That said, the killer's recent activity seems to have taken place within Hawkwood Hollow itself."

"Did you come here solely to tell me things I was already aware of?"

Her patronising tone grated on me. "I'm reminding you the killer is *here. Even* if they did start this killing spree in the normal community, they didn't learn how to summon zombies out there. They learned it here."

"Again, you're repeating what we discussed yesterday."

"I thought you might have given the matter some thought." I levelled a glare at her. "Do you have any theories about why the killer sent the zombies back to their own homes?"

Nothing about the murderer's actions made any kind of sense. Raising zombies was one thing, but sending them somewhere concerned loved ones were more likely to find them suggested the killer had *wanted* to draw attention to their crimes.

"I do not," she said. "I cannot fathom anything that goes on in the mind of someone who would commit such heinous crimes."

"Neither can I, but figuring out the killer's thought process might help us save more victims," I said. "I spoke to Tara's ghost yesterday, and she told me that she was killed somewhere outside of the town. I then spoke to the ghost of the first victim, who told me that *he* was murdered in the street here in Hawkwood Hollow."

"Your point?" she said.

"My point is that I've spoken to two ghosts who've given me contradictory information," I said. "I'd like to ask permission to summon Marilyn's ghost to break the tie and to confirm if she remembers her own death."

With a serial killer, the odds of more ghosts showing up for me to question soon enough were depressingly high, but I would have preferred not to wait for that eventuality. Marilyn's ghost hadn't appeared when I'd checked the afterworld earlier that day, so I'd need to try another method. While I might have called her ghost without bothering to consult the coven leader, I wanted to see Jennifer's reaction to my request.

"Permission?" She arched a brow. "Is that customary for a Reaper? I was under the impression you usually did as you pleased."

Did she have people reporting on me? No surprise, really.

"Just trying to keep us on the same page," I said. "I'd have already talked to her if her ghost had shown up of her own accord, like Tara's did, but as it is, I'll need to use herbs to use a summoning spell instead."

"You intend to disturb her rest, then."

"If you'd like to enlighten me of another way to find out the truth without having to wait for another victim to show up, then I'm all ears."

She gave me a cold look. "Aren't the police questioning normals for that very purpose?"

They're doing more than you are, I wanted to say. "They're doing their best, but we're looking at a killer who has access to magic beyond what the police usually deal with. And, from your reaction, beyond what the coven deals with too."

Her eyes narrowed at the slight, though I'd been positively restrained if anything. "Unlike you, I was voted into my position of authority. I didn't simply walk through the door."

"Authority?" I echoed. "Nobody voted me in as the Reaper Witch, but I'm helping out because I want to find the killer, not because it's my job."

Her *own* job was a stand-in, at least in the eyes of the not insignificant proportion of the coven who were holding out for their beloved leader's return, but I refrained from mentioning that aloud.

"Then by all means satisfy your curiosity." She indicated the door. "Good day."

I stifled an eye roll. "If you hear of another disappearance, within the coven or outside of it, then I'd appreciate it if you would please report it directly to the police."

Okay, maybe I couldn't resist getting in a last dig before I left, but I couldn't believe she had the nerve to label my concern about the killer's hideout as simple curiosity rather than a desire to prevent any further victims from being murdered and raised as the undead. It didn't help that only one of the victims so far had been a coven member, so there was a strong chance that Jennifer wouldn't have acknowledged the murders at all if Marilyn hadn't gone missing. Look at how she'd treated Tara.

Other than that, the only trait the victims obviously had in common was that they were witches or wizards. I wasn't certain whether that was a deliberate choice on the killer's part or not, but it was Drew's job to find the killer. Mine was solely to deal with the ghost-related aspect, so I left Jennifer's office and went to the storeroom downstairs to get the herbs I needed to summon a ghost the regular way without using my Reaper powers.

After leaving the coven's headquarters, I returned to the inn and picked out a spot near the river to perform the summoning. I'd selected an area under the shadow of a tall tree and out of sight of the inn, figuring it might put customers off if they saw me conducting a ghost-summoning spell on the property.

I laid out the herbs in the right formation and called Marilyn's name, but her ghost didn't appear.

"Marilyn?"

No response. I tried several more times and then used my Reaper powers to open the afterworld again for good measure, but no sign of her materialised. Sweeping away the herbs into the river, I gave up on that idea for the time being.

Had the killer banished Marilyn's ghost to keep her from talking? Or had an accomplice done it instead? Jennifer's office entered my mind's eye, and suspicion arose. She clearly knew about ghosts, given what she'd done to Mart. Blaming her for the missing ghost was my old paranoia talking, I'd freely admit, but if I had to ask if Mina Devlin would cover up for a serial killer who targeted her own coven members and turned them into zombies, I'd say yes without hesitation. I couldn't read Jennifer at all, though, and until I found proof of her wrongdoing, I'd need to put my suspicions aside for the time being.

10

Jia waved at me from behind the bar when I walked back into the restaurant. "No luck?"

I joined her, shaking my head. "Marilyn's ghost has gone walkabout and won't answer me, so she must have moved on."

"Weird," she said. "Did you try summoning her the regular way?"

"Yeah, I did," I said. "I even went to the trouble of asking Jennifer Ness's permission beforehand."

Her brows shot up. "Are you sure *she* didn't banish her ghost?"

"The thought did cross my mind," I admitted, glad I wasn't the only one with severe suspicions about the new coven leader. "Jennifer isn't the most pleasant person to deal with, but I don't know if she's actively trying to stop me from investigating. She said I could go ahead and contact Marilyn's ghost, though she seemed to think I'd claimed authority that wasn't mine by taking the case into my hands."

"As if *she* didn't claim authority when she took Mina's place."

"Exactly," I said. "She was also dismissive when I told her Drew was talking to the head of the police in the normal town nearby."

"It's his job to tell his counterpart there's a killer on the loose, right? Even in a non-magical town."

"Yeah, but he has to tell him without mentioning the zombies."

Jia gave a shudder. "At least none of the bodies from the morgue started walking around overnight."

"I wouldn't speak too soon." Drew had claimed he was waiting to hear from the morgue about autopsying the victims, but he hadn't called me yet. "They haven't done the autopsies on any of the victims yet, as far as I know, but it wouldn't surprise me if they asked me to be present in case any of the bodies inconveniently started beating people up."

She snorted. "Yeah, that would be unfortunate. I wonder how they were killed, then?"

"Mr Cogman said he got hit on the head with a blunt instrument, but I don't know about the others."

He might not have been killed by the same person, but his ghost was also nowhere to be seen. Smart of him to stay out of my way, if you asked me, but I found myself wondering if he'd spoken to any of the other victims' ghosts himself.

Come to think of it, if someone had banished Marilyn's ghost, then it was possible that they'd do the same to Mr Cogman. I wouldn't exactly shed a tear if he left, but I'd prefer to know the how and the when.

After scanning the restaurant, I flagged down one of our new ghost employees.

"Hey, Wade," I called to the older man. "Has Mr Cogman been around, do you know?"

"I saw him earlier, but he yelled at everyone to leave him alone whenever we tried to talk to him," Wade replied. "Last I saw, he was sulking in a corner of the games room."

"I'm surprised he didn't pick himself a guest room instead."

"He said none of them were suitable for his needs."

Typical. "As if he needs one anyway." I went to look in the games room, but I saw no sign of Mr Cogman in there either. That figured.

As I backed out of the room, another of our new ghostly employees drifted past.

"Hey, Jonathan," I called. "Have you seen Mr Cogman?"

"No. Has he vanished too?"

"Vanished?" I echoed. "Who's vanished?"

"Nobody I know, but I heard some of the other ghosts talking," he said. "A couple have disappeared recently."

Have they now? Spirits could move on to the next world of their own accord, of course, but if Marilyn's disappearance hadn't been natural, then I wanted to be certain there wasn't a link. "Can you let me know if anyone else disappears? I need to check in with my brother."

"Sure." He drifted away.

When I returned to the bar, Jia gave me a questioning look. "No sign of him?"

"Nope. Is Mart in there?"

"Here." My brother floated out of the kitchen. "Have fun with the coven leader?"

"Only if you substitute 'fun' with 'a tedious waste of time,'" I replied. "Mart, some of the ghosts are talking about spirits disappearing. Have you heard anything?"

"Disappearing?" he said. "Sure, they sometimes get bored hanging around and move on. Not everyone is as adept at being a ghost as I am."

"I heard someone mention a couple of missing ghosts earlier," Jia ventured. "Not unusual, is it?"

"It might be," I said. "Especially if Marilyn's ghost vanished by design. Also, Mr Cogman has gone walka-bouts again."

"He wouldn't disappear into the afterworld without raising hell on his way out," Mart said.

"You may have a point there." Still, I checked no customers were watching before calling the shadows to my hands. "Mr Cogman?"

His ghostly figure appeared at once within the dark-ness, scowling. "What?"

"I heard some other ghosts were disappearing, and I wanted to check you weren't one of them," I said. "Clearly, you're not, so feel free to go about your day. Unless you've heard any rumours of ghosts vanishing in suspicious circumstances?"

"I don't speak to the other ghosts, so I wouldn't know."

That figured. "I'd try to be nicer to them in the future if you want anyone to care if you disappear too."

Granted, he'd already pretty much blown his chances of turning over a new leaf in the afterlife, and it didn't surprise me when he disappeared into the shadows without another word.

My phone buzzed, and my heart lifted when I saw Drew's name on the screen. Answering, I said, "Hey,

Drew. How're the normals? You didn't accidentally drop any hints about our delightful and zombie-infested magical world?"

"I didn't shift into a werewolf in the middle of town, if that's what you mean."

"Ha," I said. "How did you go about explaining our zombie problem without saying the word 'zombie'?"

"I didn't," he said. "I told them there's a virus going around that's causing people to act erratically and lose control of their senses, and to let me know right away if they find anyone with those symptoms."

I snorted. "I guess that's more plausible to the normals than the alternative. Have there been any other disappearances in the region?"

"Actually… yes."

My amusement fled. "Where? How many?"

"Six or seven, mostly from the neighbouring town and villages," he said. "But it's hard to prove they might be victims of the same killer without finding the bodies."

"Or their zombies." Chills raced down my spine. Had the killer been operating for longer than any of us had known? "I guess most normals wouldn't know a zombie by sight, but the last thing we need is to have them getting suspicious."

"I doubt the killer wants to draw the normals' attention," he said. "Given that they're working from a location outside of the town's boundaries, they might not want to draw *our* attention either."

"Except for the zombies," I pointed out. "Most people in the magical world *would* know a zombie when they saw one, even if they wouldn't necessarily know how to put it down."

"Maybe, but until Mr Cogman, nobody from this town had been targeted," he said. "If not for him, we wouldn't have known at all."

"No thanks to Jennifer advising the other witches against reporting anything to the police—or to me," I added. "I spoke to her earlier, and she said there hadn't been any more disappearances. Also, she gave me permission to summon Marilyn's ghost to ask her some questions."

"How generous of her."

"Unfortunately, the spell didn't work," I said. "So we're left with two victims' ghosts who have contradictory stories. Unless… can you get me the names of any of the other victims?"

"I can try, but they're listed as missing, not dead," he said. "My team—those who were brave enough to volunteer anyway—are combing the area for the killer's hideout."

"Hope you find it."

The hideout wasn't likely to be in a place with a lot of human inhabitants, but normals were good at overlooking what was right in front of them. And if a wizard or witch was behind this, they were perfectly capable of using magic to hide in plain sight. Not to mention they could drive off any ghosts who might be able to reveal the truth too. Granted, Tara had escaped, but she hadn't been able to give us directions to the killer's lair.

"Same here," he said. "We'll also check the houses of the people in the area who were reported missing."

"In case their zombies show up," I guessed. "Let me know if you need my help with that."

Knowing my luck, I'd end up with the unenviable task

of putting down a dozen zombies without alerting a bunch of normals. Just what my week needed.

"I will," he said. "The good news is that the team at the morgue has agreed to push ahead with autopsying the bodies without delay."

"Do they need me at the morgue?"

"I did ask the team to contact you if they wanted to make sure there weren't any zombie-related issues, but it sounds like they have the situation in hand."

"Finally, some good news," I said dryly. "Speak to you later."

"Sure." He ended the call, while I wondered if the coven had somehow even convinced the people who worked at the morgue to avoid contacting me if possible. Luckily, the person who'd reanimated the bodies had stayed away while the autopsies were in process, and although I couldn't exactly complain that no one asked me to volunteer as a security guard to keep the bodies from coming back to life, I wished people would have a little faith in me for once.

As for the mysteriously disappearing ghosts… I could ask the Reaper if he'd heard anything, I supposed, but that was almost as unappealing as arm-wrestling a zombie at an autopsy.

"What are you brooding about?" Mart asked. "Upset that you can't go on a date because you're too busy wrangling the dead?"

"No." I slid my phone back in my pocket. "We have bigger problems. Turns out there have been more disappearances in the area—of normals. Unless the killer has disposed of the bodies, then their zombies might be wandering around too."

"Normals?" Jia echoed, overhearing. "Why would a serial killer target both normals and paranormals?"

"Makes about as much sense as them summoning their zombies and sending them to guard their own houses." I shook my head. "I don't much fancy the idea of going on zombie patrol in a normal village, but if the alternative is hanging out in the morgue to make sure the bodies don't attack anyone autopsying them, there's not much choice."

"Rather you than me," Mart commented. "How many more people went missing?"

"Six or seven, but some might not be the killer's victims. It's hard to know for sure when no bodies have shown up yet."

"Reanimated or otherwise, I take it," Mart added. "Speaking of which, how's the killer even summoning those zombies? There are only so many ways to learn how to reanimate someone without learning from a Reaper."

"Yeah, I know." You couldn't exactly pick it up at a night school class at the local witch academy. Even accessing a book on necromancy was unlikely without a contact. Old Harold's cottage might have a book or two on the subject, but asking him to loan them out would have been as productive as begging to borrow his scythe.

"I bet the coven had resources hidden away," Jia said thoughtfully. "I still think Jennifer Ness knows more than she let on."

"No doubt." I looked up as Carey entered the restaurant, carrying her schoolbag. "We've been neglecting our haunted hotel plan too."

"I imagine we'll have trouble finding more employees if the local spirits are disappearing," Jia remarked.

"You may have a point there." The missing ghosts

might not be connected to the murders, but the quickest way to find out would be to swallow my pride and talk to the Reaper again.

"Hey." Carey reached the bar. "Busy day?"

"For one of us," Jia said. "Maura worked this morning. I slept in. Now I'm working, and she's running around after zombies and ghosts."

"And the Reaper." I turned to Mart. "Fancy another trip to the cemetery?"

"No, I certainly wouldn't."

"Last time you got annoyed that I didn't ask you to come with me."

"That was before I found out the morgue was full of zombies."

"Zombies can't do you any harm, Mart," I reminded him. "If you ask me, old Harold is more of a hazard than a zombie."

"You've got that right," said Jia. "Give me an update when you're back."

"You're leaving already?" asked Carey.

"We're catching a killer, remember?" Jia said. "I'll tell you the latest while Maura's speaking to our resident grump of a Reaper."

"I'll be back soon." I'd already filled Carey in on yesterday's misadventures, including my meeting with the new coven leader accompanied by Drew and our failed attempt to find Marilyn at her own house. Jia would have to tell her the rest while I spoke to the Reaper.

This time I took a shortcut through the shadows and landed directly in front of old Harold's cottage. Generally, I tended to keep that kind of thing to a minimum to avoid startling people, but my Reaper status wasn't a big secret to him, and if I was wasting my time, I'd prefer not to go to the trouble of walking all the way to his house.

One rap on the door brought the usual response: "Go away."

"Have any ghosts been disappearing?" I asked Harold through the closed door. "Except in the usual way, that is?"

"I wouldn't know. I haven't spoken to any."

"You see them." Why had I thought this guy would be any help again? Oh, right, I hadn't. "The ghost of the latest murder victim didn't show up even when I tried a witch-style summoning spell. Now I'm hearing more ghosts are vanishing without warning too."

"Maybe your powers are defective."

"Low blow, Harold." I did not appreciate the reminder of the coven's antics a few weeks ago in which they'd sneakily hit me with a spell and led me to believe my Reaper powers were malfunctioning—and the old Reaper's comments about that had not helped in the slightest. "It might have escaped your attention, but there's a serial killer in town who also happens to be raising their victims from the dead. I don't suppose you have any books on the subject of summoning the dead, or necromancy in general?"

"Not if the person responsible isn't a Reaper."

"Is that true?" I looked at the door suspiciously. "You'd tell me if there was another Reaper around... wouldn't you?"

Silence.

"Harold. Let's not do this again."

"Yes, I'd tell you," he growled, with obvious reluctance. "Now, go away."

I breathed out. "It's not a Reaper, so it must be a witch or wizard, as I originally thought."

"That's the logical conclusion."

Hmm. Reading between the lines told me he'd been thinking on the matter himself. I'd known the guy wasn't *completely* indifferent to what went on in town, even if he did have an annoying habit of not telling me of important information. That didn't make said habit any less annoying, though.

"I assume you'll tell me if you hear anything of note, from either the dead or the living?" I queried. "Or do I need to check in on you?"

"Do I need to get out my scythe?"

"Lovely to see you too." I turned away, shaking my head. He'd at least confirmed that the murders weren't a Reaper's work, but I was as much in the dark as ever about the killer's actual identity.

As I left the cemetery, my phone buzzed with a call from Drew. "Hey," I answered. "On your way back yet?"

"Yes, I just got back to Hawkwood Hollow," he said. "The team at the morgue called me with the results of the autopsies and told me to come straight back. I think you ought to hear them too."

Oh, boy. That didn't sound like good news. "I'll be right there."

I veered down the road towards the morgue, looking around for Drew. He showed up within minutes, looking windswept but better put together than one might expect of someone who must have been running around in wolf form shortly beforehand. Given the timing, the only way for him to have got back into town so fast was if he'd shifted into his werewolf form.

Almost as handy as using the shadows as a shortcut like I did.

"You moved fast," he commented.

"Speak for yourself," I replied. "I was talking to a certain friendly Reaper when you called me. Anyway, what's the news from the morgue?"

"The victims were killed with magic," he said. "The spell didn't leave a mark, which I suspect was an intentional choice on the part of the caster, but the people who did the autopsies suspect a ritual was used to kill both victims."

My heart dropped. "I was afraid you were going to say that."

I was pretty sure raising someone from death as a zombie required a ritual itself. My knowledge on the subject was rusty, but rituals were generally used to generate energy and direct it towards a given purpose. Sacrificing a person's life was a fast way to generate a lot of magical power, but this killer had sacrificed multiple lives. What had they been trying to do? And why and how had their victims ended up rising from the grave?

"I thought so," Drew said. "You know more about this kind of thing than I do."

"Not enough," I murmured. "They don't teach it in Reaper training, no more than the basic theory, and I never paid much attention anyway. Reapers don't need to resort to those methods to raise the dead when we have the afterworld at our fingertips already."

"Did you think old Harold might have an idea where they learned?" he asked.

"I asked if he had any books, but he said he only had the sort aimed at Reapers, not regular people." I shook my head. "As for the coven... for all I know, Mina took anything useful with her, but that's speculation on my part."

"It's a good enough guess," said Drew. "It's possible the coven does have resources, but now we've finally established a working relationship with them, I'd prefer not to jeopardise it by making unfounded accusations."

"It's not much of a working relationship, given how little effort Jennifer has put into helping me." I shook my head. "And the other victims are normals, so she'll probably wash her hands of the matter unless another coven member goes missing."

His expression darkened. "The normals started disappearing more than a week ago. This has been going on for longer than we were aware."

"It's a tough one." Movement stirred in the corner of my eye. "Hang on. We're being watched."

I turned sharply to the left and spied a figure backing away hastily. Not a ghost. Swiftly, I strode over to him before he could run off. "Mr White?"

Ellis White blinked at me. "I'm sorry. I didn't mean to intrude."

"What are you doing here?"

"I wanted to know what happened to Alan." He indicated the morgue. "I know they took his body in..."

My suspicion rose. "And you happened to drop by right when the results of his autopsy came out, did you?"

He blanched. "I didn't know."

"Not just him," I added. "There were other victims of the same serial killer too. Know anything about them?"

He shook his head. "No, not at all. A serial killer? Was that who killed him?"

"Looks that way." Being killed in a ritual in a secret lair was a world away from being hit over the head in the street, but who had killed Mr Cogman if not the same person who'd raised the others from the dead? Mr White's habit of showing up in suspicious places didn't prove his own guilt, but his claims of ignorance didn't ring true.

He swallowed. "Ah, Reaper Witch, I'm sorry I disturbed you. I hope you find the murderer."

"As do I," Drew added from next to me. "I trust you'll let me know if you have any information, Mr White."

"Yes. Of course." He turned away from the morgue, and I watched him leave through narrowed eyes.

"I don't trust him."

"I thought you'd say that," said Drew. "I can't say he looks much like the serial killer type to me."

"It's always the ones you least expect." Not that this guy was at the bottom of my suspect list. I refused to believe he'd dropped by here by accident, any more than his visit to Mr Cogman's house had been coincidental.

I think it might be time for a chat with Mr Cogman about his "friend."

11

M art accosted me when I entered the inn.

"What's the verdict?" he asked. "Did any of the bodies come back to life?"

"Nope, but the theory is that they were all killed in a ritual—with one exception," I said. "Is Mr Cogman around?"

"I saw him a minute ago," he said. "I may have insulted him a little. What kind of ritual?"

"A nasty one, considering how many people they killed." *And it's not even over yet.* "I'll tell you the rest after I find Mr Cogman."

I headed for the games room, somewhat surprised to spot him drifting in a corner, glowering at the wall as if it had mortally offended him.

"You again," he said. "I'm glad you had the courtesy to find me in person rather than disturbing me without warning."

"Because you've obviously got so much else going on

in your afterlife." I rolled my eyes. "I thought you'd want to know I saw your friend at the morgue earlier."

"Who?"

"Mr White. He seemed interested in the result of your autopsy."

"You performed an autopsy on my body?" His eyes narrowed, while his voice rose in volume.

Oops. I should probably have refrained from mentioning that part. "I didn't do it myself. The authorities wanted to confirm how you died…"

"Without asking my permission first!" he spluttered with indignation. "I might be dead, but I still have rights."

"That's not how it works."

He shot across the room like a transparent bullet, straight through the wall. I ran in pursuit, swearing under my breath. This was all I needed—a runaway ghost with entirely too much autonomy.

"Get back here." In the reception area, I caught up to him and grabbed his arm. He felt disconcertingly solid for a ghost—except for when he slithered through my grip and escaped through the doors.

Oh, no you don't. The patrons of the restaurant, both living and dead, stared at me through the window as I ran across the bridge in pursuit of the ghost.

"Seriously!" I panted, reaching the other side of the river. "You're several hours too late to stop the autopsy now."

Ignoring me, he flew on until he came to a halt at the morgue. Briefly, I wondered how he'd even figured out where it was, but of course he'd been a *living* resident of Hawkwood Hollow until recently. However hard it was to imagine him as anything other than a cranky ghost.

I skidded to a halt, bent double to catch my breath. "There's nothing you can do. If you get your body out of there, what exactly did you plan to do with it?"

He didn't answer. When he drifted closer to the morgue, I grabbed his arm from behind and attempted to drag him back, which was as effective as trying to move a block of concrete with my bare hands.

Then, mid-tussle, I noticed we weren't alone. To my disconcertion, Mr White still hovered near the fence, as if he'd hoped that if he stood there for long enough, someone would give him the autopsy report. His confused gaze followed my movements as I tried to stop Mr Cogman breaking free.

"Mind helping me out?" I called to him. "Your friend's ghost is trying to get into the morgue."

"He's not my friend," Mr Cogman supplied.

"Is he?" Mr White asked, not hearing his reply. "I... can't see ghosts. Sorry."

Right. Of course he couldn't. "I told him about the autopsy, and he got all offended at the idea of someone cutting up his corpse."

"Oh," he said. "Yes, understandable. I'd talk sense into him, but…"

"But he doesn't *have* any sense to begin with." I lost my grip on Mr Cogman, who flew up to the morgue door and came to an abrupt halt. I'd forgotten about the sage the police had put outside the door. *Good. That ought to keep him out.*

Freed from my ghostly burden, I turned to Mr White. "What are you still doing here, exactly?"

"This won't stand!" Mr Cogman bellowed at the morgue door. Nobody answered him.

Mr White flushed and looked down. "As I told you earlier... I got curious."

"So you decided to stick around in the hopes that someone would let you in." I grimaced at Mr Cogman's shouting in the background. "Be glad you can't hear the racket he's making."

"What does he expect them to do?"

"I honestly don't know." I'd hoped to ask Mr White some more questions about his potential involvement in the murders but not in front of one of the victims. Even when the guy couldn't see the ghost, the noise was starting to give me a headache.

"Why not put him in his *own* house?" Mr White suggested. "You can trap a ghost using sage, right? That's what's keeping him out?"

"Been researching, have you?"

"No, everyone learns that at school. Don't they?"

True enough, but coming from him, the casual comment hit a different note. If he couldn't see ghosts, then it was hard to see him being responsible for their disappearances, but I still didn't trust him.

Either way, it wouldn't be wise to let Mr Cogman's ghost out of my sight. Once he'd moved on, my chances of asking him more questions would plummet to zero. On the other hand, confining him to the inn within a circle of sage risked scaring off other ghosts too.

"Let me in!" Mr Cogman shouted at the morgue door.

Honestly, one ghost wasn't worth this much trouble. Raising my voice so that both Mr Cogman and his friend could hear me, I said, "Not everyone learns how to conduct ritualistic killings, though."

Mr Cogman wasn't even paying attention, but Mr

White took a startled step back at my words. "Ritualistic killings? That... that wasn't how he died?"

"Not him but the killer's other victims." I watched his expression carefully, though it was hard to tell whether his horror came from the revelation that his friend had been sacrificed in a ritual or the fear that I'd figured him out. "Yes, there were several, though your friend broke the killer's pattern in a few ways."

Mr White simply looked confused. "I don't understand."

"He wasn't sacrificed, and he was killed here in Hawkwood Hollow, not at the same location as the other victims," I explained. "A location we have yet to find. Which I'm sure you figured out if you've been eavesdropping on the police as well as on the morgue."

He flinched. "I didn't... I wasn't trying to probe into the investigation. I was concerned for a friend, that's all."

"He already told me he's not your friend." I watched Mr Cogman out of the corner of my eye as he floated to the other side of the morgue, continuing to yell at the building as he did so. "I find it hard to believe he has any, come to that. He seems to hate everyone."

Mr White shook his head. "No. He rarely holds a grudge, except perhaps against that neighbour of his."

"You mean Simon?"

"That's him," Mr White said. "He's always trying to needle him. If ever I was to suspect anyone of wrongdoing, it would be him."

"He seemed perfectly normal when the police questioned him," I said. "In fact, he was even concerned for his neighbour, despite your friend's severe attitude problems. Hardly serial killer material."

"You only met him once," he said.

"And you know him as well as Mr Cogman, do you?" Why Mr White would leap to the defence of a person as pleasant as a fungus-infected toe was beyond me. Unless he was attempting to deflect my suspicions that *he'd* murdered his so-called friend. He couldn't seek the approval of a ghost he couldn't actually see, after all, and Mr Cogman himself seemed utterly indifferent to him.

"Every time I went to see him, Alan and I caught him peering at us through a gap in the curtains when he thought we weren't looking," he said. "He's not as innocent as he appears."

"Nosiness doesn't make someone a serial murderer," I told him. "As it happens, the first few victims weren't even from Hawkwood Hollow, and the killer isn't operating from within the town itself."

He blinked. "How interesting."

"I'd use the word 'disturbing' before 'interesting,' personally. But it's true." I folded my arms across my chest. "You should know I'm not *technically* supposed to discuss these things with suspects, but I wanted to hear your thoughts."

"Suspects?" His mouth turned down at the corners. "I'm not... a suspect, am I?"

"Since you turned up in Mr Cogman's house when his zombie was inside and now you're trying to get into the morgue—yes."

He frowned. "I told you, I was there out of concern for Alan, nothing more."

"Stop talking about me as if I'm not here!" Mr Cogman, having apparently abandoned his quest to get into the morgue by the force of will alone, appeared behind Mr White.

"I didn't think you were paying any attention." I rolled my eyes at him. "Finished your temper tantrum, then?"

"I…" Mr White trailed off. "Wait, is Alan talking to you right now?"

"Yes, he is." I nodded to Mr Cogman. "Ready to stop sulking and come back to the inn?"

"I most certainly am not sulking," Mr Cogman snapped. "Nor will I stand for being ordered around."

"You're safer with me than you are elsewhere, like it or not."

"What?" Mr White said. "Why would that be? He's a ghost, isn't he? Nobody can threaten a ghost."

"I can," I corrected, "but that's not the point I'm making. You're a suspect, and I'm here to pick up Mr Cogman, not play mind games with you."

"I didn't know that was what we were doing," Mr White said. "Regardless, I think Simon has more to say that he hasn't shared with the police."

"I think you have more to share with the police yourself," I said. "If you're genuinely concerned, go and talk to them."

"I'm not coming with you," Mr Cogman said flatly.

"I thought you wanted to stay at the inn until I helped solve your murder." Conversing with a ghost and a living person at the same time required a level of finesse I did not have the energy for at the moment. "You insisted on it, in fact."

"You haven't done a thing for me," he growled. "You've done nothing but treat me like a liability."

"If you didn't act like one, then I wouldn't need to," I

said. "I seem to remember saying I'd send you to the afterworld the next time you crossed me, but here I am, giving you a second chance."

"Then I'll take my leave of you." Mr Cogman spun on his heel and vanished into the shadows.

"Great." I dropped my hands. "That's that done, then."

"What's done?" Mr White asked. "Wait… he's gone?"

"Not permanently." *More's the pity.* Theoretically, I could grab him from the afterworld and drag him back to the inn, but that would require a level of patience I didn't possess. "Feel free to go looking for him yourself."

I didn't wait to hear Mr White's reply. If he wanted to hang around the morgue all day in the hopes that someone would take pity on him, then it'd serve him right if he got arrested. I messaged Drew telling him that Mr White was *still* there, but really, he had better things to do than to deal with him when he had a killer to catch.

Unless Mr White himself was the killer we'd been looking for… but despite his seemingly baseless accusations towards Mr Cogman's neighbour, I wasn't certain he was the murderer. Not least because his inability to see ghosts would hinder any kind of necromantic rituals.

Irked, I headed back to the inn and found Carey sitting at her usual table, talking to Jia behind the bar.

"There you are," Carey said when she saw me. "Mum said you ran out of here earlier."

"Our delightful ghost decided to run to the morgue to protest against his autopsy."

"Oh." She wrinkled her nose. "Did you catch him?"

"Yeah, but he slipped away again, so I decided to leave him be for the time being."

I knew how to pick my battles, after all.

"He left?" asked Jia from behind the bar. "You think he might disappear?"

"He'd be doing everyone else in the town a favour if he did." I shook my head. "It's lucky the police put sage around the morgue, or else he'd be in there stirring up trouble instead of on the outside. If I want to find him again, I'll use the afterworld. It's that or confine him to the inn, and it's not worth putting off our new employees by dropping sage everywhere."

"That's fair," she said. "So… was anything unexpected revealed in the autopsy?"

"The victims were all killed with magic, except for Mr Cogman," I said. "A spell that left no mark on them. The team at the morgue thinks it was a ritual."

Her brows shot up. "Mr Cogman too?"

"No, he said he was struck behind with a blunt instrument," I said. "In the street, not in the killer's lair. It was why I figured letting him go wasn't the worst idea. The other victims' ghosts are more likely to have a useful perspective on where the killer is hiding, and for all I know, someone else killed Mr Cogman in the first place."

"True," she said. "A ritual, though? Was it the same one that raised them as zombies?"

"Possibly, but I don't know *why* someone would go to that much trouble if all they wanted was a bunch of mindless drones to obey their every whim. Why not just raise bodies who were already dead rather than creating their own?"

"Yeah… that doesn't add up," she said. "If they used a ritual to kill that many victims, then they had a specific goal. A big one."

"I don't think we should be using the past tense here," I

said. "The murders are ongoing. We don't know how many other victims there are either."

"True," she said. "The killer planned this from the outset, I'm guessing. Question is, who is it?"

"Well, right now I have Mr White tied with the coven at the top of my list of suspects."

"Wow," she said. "What did this Mr White do to deserve being tied with the coven?"

"First he showed up at Mr Cogman's house when I was dealing with his zombie and pretended it was a coincidence," I answered. "Then he showed up at the morgue to find out the results of the autopsy—and sneaked back over there as soon as I was gone."

"That's persistent," she said. "Who was he again? A colleague?"

"Or so *he* said, but I don't know." I shook my head. "He claimed they were friends, but Mr Cogman disagreed with that assessment. Mr White can't see or hear ghosts, so he didn't have to listen to his ranting, but it doesn't sound like they agree on their friendship status."

"Awkward," she said.

"Tell me about it," I said. "Anyway, I sent him packing, but I bet he'll be straight back to the morgue when he thinks I'm gone. I want Drew to give him a proper questioning, but he's up to his neck in complaints about zombies."

"Yeah, questioning that guy is Drew's job," she said. "I have no idea who he is, so I can't say I have an opinion on him either way. The coven's still at the top of my list."

Was he the killer? The coven had occupied the top spot on my own list until now, and I remained irked at Jennifer's utter lack of any help, but they'd done nothing to implicate themselves in this case directly. Not compared to Mr White.

"You think the coven might be covering for murderers again?" asked Carey.

"I do," Jia said. "Is this Mr White guy linked to the coven in any way?"

"Not that I'm aware of, but they don't let wizards apply," I said. "Doesn't mean he isn't involved, though. Even Mina Devlin rarely committed any crimes herself."

Except the floods over two decades ago, for which nobody had ever faced justice. Few even suspected Mina might have been involved aside from Harold and me. The Reaper had confirmed my suspicions but ordered me to avoid confronting the coven without proof and then returned to his habit of avoiding the subject. If the current situation had been connected to that debacle, I might have had an easier job gaining his cooperation, but he generally refused to lift a finger to help anyone, dead or alive.

Jia's expression shadowed. "It honestly wouldn't surprise me if this was her work too. She's up to no good even if she isn't in town."

"I don't doubt she is."

But for all that, I couldn't shake the feeling that if Mina was in the area, there would have been more signs. Most of her supporters were in jail, and if she wanted to take power back, she'd have to either instigate a jailbreak or bring enough supporters into the fold to rebuild the coven from scratch. Neither of those things was impossible, but I could think of zero connection between her and Mr Cogman. Or Mr Cogman and anyone else either, except for the mile-long list of people he'd annoyed.

I desperately hoped I hadn't made a mistake in sending

away his ghost, because I was starting to wonder if he'd been an intended victim at all. He might have been turned into a zombie, but he hadn't been near the site of the ritual that had killed the others. Had he been a witness? Or was he just an unlucky bystander who'd been caught in the aftermath? If so, then why was Mr White so adamant that Simon was involved in his death? Aside from the obvious: to deflect from his own culpability in the murders…

My phone buzzed with a reply from Drew telling me the police had contacted Mr White to come in for an interview the next day. *Good.*

However reluctant he might be to talk, we'd get him to spill his secrets one way or another.

12

When Jia showed up at work the next day, she brought another ghost for an interview. The spirit, a middle-aged woman named Louise, had a talent for making windows and doors rattle in time to music. Handy enough for a ghost tour, though of course it gave Mart a new way to annoy me all morning. At least the two of them kept us all entertained while I waited for Drew to tell me about his interview with Mr White that day.

Typically, when he did call back, we were dealing with an influx of lunchtime customers. Jia stepped in and took over from me at the counter, and I shot her a grateful nod as I went to take the call.

"Hey," I said to Drew. "Have you talked to Mr White yet?"

"No... there's been another development," he said. "I thought you'd want to know Mr Cogman's neighbour has been arrested."

"Not Simon?" *Was that Mr White's doing?* "Didn't I tell you Mr White was trying to pin the blame on the guy?"

"My team found evidence in his house suggesting his involvement in Mr Cogman's death." He sounded tired. "If you're able to get away from work, then you should come and have a look for yourself."

I glanced over at the bar, where Jia gave me a thumbs-up, letting me know she had the situation in hand. I still felt a stab of guilt for leaving her, but if Simon had really been found with incriminating evidence, then I wanted to see it with my own eyes.

"All right," I said. "I'll be right there."

Of all the complications that might have arisen from the police questioning Mr White, I hadn't guessed that they'd arrest Simon instead. *He didn't put them up to it, did he?* Or was this the coven's doing instead? To find out, I needed to talk to Drew, so I ended the call and returned to the bar.

"I have to go," I murmured to Jia. "I'll be back as soon as I can."

"What happened?" Mart stopped playing the *Star Wars* theme on the blinds and drifted into view.

"Supposedly, the police found evidence against Mr Cogman's neighbour," I told him and Jia. "Simon, the dude Mr White was accusing yesterday with zero proof to back it up. I'll have to go there in person to see what they found, exactly, but I'm not buying it."

Jia frowned. "You think someone set him up?"

"There's a fair chance," I said. "I'm sorry for running off again, but—"

"If it's to stop an innocent man's arrest, I can forgive

you." She waved me off. "Go on, ask Allie. I'm more than happy to cover for you for a bit."

"Thanks." I ran to find Allie and repeated the same story to her, and she agreed to let me take time out to deal with this unexpected setback.

"Drew's sensible, and so are you," she said. "You'll get this sorted. I have faith in you."

Hoping her faith wasn't misplaced, I thanked her and left the inn. Ordinarily, I might have used the shadows as a shortcut, but it would not endear me to the officers if I jumped out of the afterworld and accidentally landed on top of them.

Instead, I ran. After crossing the bridge, I turned onto Mr Cogman's street in time to see two officers leading Simon out of his house. His expression was stunned and dazed, and he made no effort to resist.

Nearby, Drew saw me and gave a smile as tired as his voice had sounded on the phone. "Maura, did you run all the way here?"

"How can you tell?" I bent double to catch my breath. "What made you decide to search Simon's house?"

"We always planned to question the neighbours again," he said. "Simon happened to be at the top of the list."

"But... Mr White." He was supposed to be their priority, wasn't he? "Wasn't he meant to show up to be interviewed this morning?"

"He was, but we had to postpone the interview when one of my officers called me back to Simon's house after he found... well, judge for yourself."

I gave him a questioning look. "I'm allowed in?"

"Of course," he answered. "If you look around his house, you might see something none of us picked up on."

"Like a ghost?" I assumed no dead bodies were in there, at any rate, so I followed him towards the house. Outside the door, a female officer with curly dark hair and glasses gave me a distrusting look, to which I responded with a fake smile. "Hey, there. Drew said I can look around."

"I did," Drew told the officer. "Maura is here to look for any other clues that we might have overlooked."

"So I heard." The officer didn't look happy in the slightest, but she moved aside to let me enter the house.

The hallway in front of us mirrored the one in the house next door, down to the trapdoor, which lay wide open. Next to it sat a heap of inexplicable objects—hair clips, jewellery, even a shoe or two. None looked like they might have belonged to Simon, unless he had a secret wife stashed away unbeknownst to us.

"What...?" I trailed off as the penny dropped. "Who did those belong to?"

"The victims—that is, some belonged to Tara and Marilyn," said Drew from behind me. "Others we aren't sure of, but given the other disappearances in the area, there's a fair chance that when I talk to the officers in the neighbouring town, I'll be able to return them to their families."

Nausea rushed through me. "You really think Simon killed them? Did you find any signs of—of a ritual or anything?"

"No," he said. "My officers have yet to find the place the murders were committed, but it's not implausible that he killed them elsewhere and then brought the trophies back to his house."

"Did he seem like the sort to commit murder, let alone

collect trophies belonging to his victims?" I surveyed the heap of objects. "Were they just lying in the cellar? Nothing else in there?"

"Nothing, except a few empty boxes. Simon claims he doesn't use the cellar for anything but storage and that he hadn't been inside in months."

That sounded more plausible than him secretly being a serial killer, but I'd bet his officers wouldn't take my word for it on that.

"Can I look down there?" I approached the trapdoor. Someone had leaned a ladder against the edge of the square hole in the floor, but the cellar itself remained cast in darkness.

"Of course," Drew said in a low voice. "For the record, I'm not sure this is as conclusive as it looks, but not everyone can see what you can, Maura."

Exactly. I pulled out my wand and cast a light charm to make sure I wasn't about to unwittingly climb into a ritualistic summoning circle or anything. The floor looked unmarked, though, so I clambered down the ladder.

As Drew had said, the cellar was empty except for a few empty boxes. No evidence whatsoever of nefarious activities. The place didn't even smell like magic, and most herbal concoctions used in ritual magic lingered in the air for days afterwards. More crucially, no ghosts were drifting around.

Shadows came to my hands, and I addressed the afterworld in general. "Anyone there?"

Nobody answered.

"Marilyn?" I called out. "Tara?"

Silence. I didn't know the other victims' names, so as a last resort, I called Mr Cogman's name. It was more of a relief than an annoyance when he didn't show up, given his irrational dislike of his neighbour, but without ghostly evidence one way or the other, the police would take the objects as definite proof of Simon's guilt.

Resigned, I pushed the shadows away and climbed out of the cellar. I touched down in the hallway.

"Find anything?" asked Drew.

I shook my head. "Nope, but if that guy's a murderer, I'm a unicorn."

Drew glanced at the heap of objects next to the open trapdoor. "Then how did they get into his house? He claims he didn't hear anyone break in."

"I can think of a dozen spells to enable someone to silently enter a house, and I'm not even that good of a witch," I said. "Trust me, it's far more likely that Mr White got in through a secret tunnel or something and planted the evidence."

"There's no secret tunnel," he said. "Or any other traces of magic, though I haven't been able to send in a witch or wizard from the team to double-check."

"Let me guess, they're avoiding zombies," I said. "Of which there are none. Besides, the guy's innocent."

The female officer from outside stuck her head in through the open doorway. "Are you quite finished nosing around the crime scene?"

"I'm going to assume you're talking to me and not your boss," I said. "For the record, I found zero evidence that any dark magic was used in that cellar or that any murders were committed on the property."

"That's for us to determine, not you," she said. "Besides, according to the autopsy reports, the murders were committed using magic, which doesn't always leave traces."

"Rituals certainly do." I sensed I was fighting a losing battle with this one, so I walked the short distance to the door and stepped out of the house.

Several more police officers had gathered outside, while the female officer frowned at me. "Whether the murders were committed on the property or not is irrelevant. Even if we do find a hidden property outside of the town as the ghost you spoke to allegedly claimed, that doesn't preclude Simon's involvement."

Allegedly, huh. If I had to guess, she didn't think a ghost's word was proof enough, and the police's failure to find the elusive killer's lair must be trying their patience too. No wonder they'd leapt on this so-called proof.

"I can give you several reasons it isn't possible for Simon to have killed those people," I said. "Firstly, you'd think someone else on the street would have noticed him going back and forth from a lair outside of the town."

"Like Mr Cogman." She indicated his house next door. "Drew tells me that you said Mr Cogman's ghost expressed distrust towards his neighbour. Perhaps Simon killed him to ensure his silence."

I stifled a snort. "Mr Cogman's ghost is the exact opposite of silent. He also told me that he didn't know anything about the other murder victims or how they died. He disliked Simon, true, but he didn't give any concrete reasons to connect him with the murders."

"The objects we found in his cellar are reason enough," said the officer. "As for the bodies, we'll keep searching."

"We will," Drew said, "and if we find proof to the contrary, Simon will be released from custody."

He'd better be. The evidence was damning, yes, but we had zero proof that it'd been placed there by Simon himself. The trouble was that the officers evidently wanted to tie up this case and wash their hands of ever having to deal with zombies again, but it didn't for a minute mean the killer wasn't still out there.

I glanced towards Simon, who shot a pleading look in my direction, but the officers continued to lead him away without acknowledging my presence.

"I don't believe he's guilty," I said, raising my voice a little. "Even if he is, the murders almost certainly didn't take place in this house, so you still have a location to find that might contain the bodies of the victims. Don't think this is over."

Drew caught my gaze and said in a low voice, "He'll get a fair trial and a chance to plead innocent. I can give him that."

"But your other officers have already made up their minds." And Drew risked losing their respect if he let Simon walk free based on my word alone. Proving Simon's innocence required finding indisputable evidence that could stand up against a pile of the victims' own possessions found in his cellar, which seemed a tall order when we didn't even *know* most of the victims. That Drew had let me walk around the crime scene hadn't helped matters, either, but this was hardly the first time I'd had to go against the authorities to reach the truth.

Drew's mouth turned downward. "Are you sure the ghosts aren't talking?"

"Not here, at any rate." I exhaled in a sigh. "I haven't seen Mr Cogman today yet, but knowing him, he'll throw a party when I tell him that Simon got arrested."

"Might be worth asking him a couple of questions," he murmured. "To be certain."

"Yeah." I stepped away and called the shadows to my hands. "Mr Cogman."

No response came.

"Mr Cogman, seriously. Get over here." I peered into the darkness and brought his face into my mind's eye. "Mr Cogman. *Alan.*"

He didn't answer. A chill raced through me. While I repeated his name until Drew gently rested a hand on my shoulder, I knew for sure that he'd gone.

On my way back to the inn, I ran into Carey walking back from school. I'd opted not to follow the officers back to the station, since I saw no sense in arguing in Simon's defence without any proof, so I hurried to catch her up. "Hey."

Slowing her pace, she smiled. "Hey, Maura. Busy day?"

I exhaled in a sigh. "Yeah, you might say that."

Her face fell. "Bad news?"

"They arrested the wrong man." I reached the doors to the inn first, which slid open. "And nobody seems to believe his innocence except for Drew and me. Worse, Mr Cogman has vanished."

"And that's supposed to be bad news?" said Mart, over-hearing as we walked into the restaurant.

"It isn't... and it is." I rubbed my forehead. "He would disappear the one time I actually need him around. I shouldn't have let him out of my sight, but I didn't know his neighbour would get arrested."

Carey's jaw dropped. "What... Drew arrested his neighbour? Really?"

"Based on evidence, but I don't think Simon himself is the one who put it there," I explained. "In his cellar, the police found objects belonging to the victims. No bodies or anything, no traces of dark magic... just a heap of random items that anyone might have planted there to frame him."

"Who do you think did it, then?" Mart drifted in front of me. "Mr Cogman can't have. He's a ghost."

"Mr White is very much alive. And he was supposed to be questioned by the police this morning if not for the convenient interruption."

Carey's eyes widened. "You think he planted the evidence? How?"

"He's a wizard. He might have gone about it in a dozen ways. Simon didn't hear a break-in, but that's hardly proof."

"Drew has wizards on his team, doesn't he?" Carey asked. "Can't they trace whether magic was used in the house recently?"

"Yes, but I think most of them were traumatised over the incident with the zombie and haven't returned to look around the house," I said. "They're also searching the fields for the killer's lair, so they're spread pretty thin. Even if Simon *is* guilty, he didn't commit the murders in his own house. The hideout is still out there somewhere."

The question was, who had sent Mr Cogman's ghost away? Mr White couldn't even *see* him, but at this point, all bets were off. I couldn't shake the feeling that I'd screwed up by not strong-arming our ghost into coming back to the inn and making him stay there regardless of how much chaos he caused.

Carey looked me over. "It's not your fault, Maura."

She was perceptive enough to guess my train of thought, but I wasn't sure she was right this time. I hadn't exactly handled Mr Cogman with grace, even if he did have the worst personality on this side of the grave.

I headed to the bar at the back of the restaurant, where Jia, I belatedly noticed, was flanked by two ghosts. One was our new employee, Louise, and the other was a tall male ghost I didn't know.

"Jia made a new friend," Mart told me. "She seems to pick them up everywhere she goes. Possibly because she has a nicer personality than yours."

"Oi."

Jia waved at me. "Hey, Maura. Hey, Carey. Meet our new employees."

"You already hired another one?"

"Yep." She indicated the male ghost on her right. "This is Brian. Maura already met Louise, who's been entertaining us by making the windows rattle all day, right?"

"Right." I addressed Carey. "If you hear the blinds rattling in time to the *Star Wars* theme, you know who to blame."

Carey smiled in the ghosts' general direction. "Nice to meet you both."

"What can you do?" I asked the new ghost.

"This." Brian raised his hands, and the temperature dropped. Ice began to spring up on the windows, and beer froze in the glasses Jia was pouring.

"Whoa." I shivered. "You might want to tone that down before we get customer complaints."

"Sorry." He gave me a sheepish look. "I've mostly been using it to prank people, so I'm still learning to apply moderation."

"Hey, it's all good for our ghost tours," I said. "If you keep it in reserve, you can apply it to one of our more annoying customers as well."

Two new ghosts in one day? Disappearances aside, word must have begun to spread among the local spirits that we were hiring.

"We almost have enough to start proper tours," Carey said enthusiastically, as if she'd sensed my thoughts. "We should do a trial run first."

I raised a brow. "Not sure our guests would want to take part."

Our only current guests were an elderly couple who'd come on a walking holiday, possibly having confused Hawkwood Hollow with somewhere else. I didn't want us to be liable for frightening anyone to death.

Allie walked over to greet her daughter. "Good day?"

"Yes," she answered. "Especially now Jia and Maura have hired two more ghosts."

"Jia did all the work," I corrected. "But yeah, we have five now."

"Enough for a real tour," Carey added. "Can we have a trial run? Tonight?"

"Of course we can." Allie beamed. "That's great news."

At least one thing had gone right this week, and I didn't have much else to do that evening after Mr Cogman's inconveniently timed disappearance. Besides, we'd been working towards this for ages, and I didn't need to ruin Carey's mood and let her down on top of everything else.

Allie peered at my face. "Are you okay, Maura?"

"Yes, I am." She was as perceptive as her daughter, but I didn't need to spend the night feeling sorry for myself *and* poor Simon for being stuck in jail. If anything, I could use the distraction. "The tour is a good idea."

"I know you hoped to see Drew soon," she said. "Is he still busy?"

"Yeah, half his team is still searching the fields," I said. "He's going to be dealing with false alarms about zombies for a while too."

"No thanks." She gave a shudder. "I'd prefer to keep those out of my inn."

"Same here." Leaving her to ask Carey about her school day, I went through the automatic doors connecting the restaurant to the inn, debating grabbing some props and trying a summoning spell as a last-ditch effort to find Mr Cogman before I threw in the towel.

"You're moping." My brother followed me into the lobby. "I can tell."

I turned to Mart. "Aren't you bothered that an innocent man is in jail and our serial killer is walking free?"

"Sure, but there's nothing I can do," he said. "Same with you, so you don't need to spend the rest of the day sulking."

"Mr Cogman is the expert on sulking, not me," I pointed out. "Or should that be *was* the expert? Would you believe I wish I'd kept him in here?"

"At least now I'm the most interesting ghost at the inn again."

I rolled my eyes at him. "You know, I've got to hand it to the real killer for covering all his bases and dropping evidence in Simon's cellar of all places. I wonder if Mr

White will actually show up at the police station at all, or if they'll give up on questioning him entirely?"

I could theoretically jump to his side this instant, if I wanted to, but that would only end in embarrassment if I didn't catch him in the act of doing anything incriminating. Besides, it was too late to spare Simon a night in jail, so I'd need to have some patience until the real evidence appeared.

As long as they kept combing the area, the police would find the killer's secret lair eventually, along with the bodies of the other victims. Wouldn't they?

13

When the last customer had left the restaurant at the end of the evening's shift, we prepared to set up our ghost tour trial run. Thanks to Carey's unrelenting enthusiasm, even I'd put the serial killer in the back of my mind and got into the mood. Allie, Jia, and I agreed to be test subjects for the trial run, while the ghosts dispersed throughout the inn according to Carey's instructions.

"Here we go." She bounded into the lobby. "I've spent all week designing the schedule. Now all we need is a test run."

"With us as the guinea pigs." Jia grinned. "Hey—Mart, stay back."

"You aren't kicking me out?" He huffed.

"No, but the focus is on the other ghosts for now," I said. "You can live without being the centre of attention for one evening, can't you?"

"Technically, I can't live with *or* without anything." He pouted. "Fine, fine."

As he drifted away, we started at the lobby door and waited for Carey to kick off the tour.

"Mart, you can mess around in the background if you like," she called to him—though addressing the wall instead of Mart himself. "Just don't trip us up or do anything too outrageous."

Mart gave a salute and flew off, and Carey turned to the rest of us. "Ready?"

"You bet," said Jia.

"You'll do great," Allie encouraged her. "Let's go."

The tour began with Carey leading the way through the lobby, where Vicky lurked in a corner waiting to grab the hands of unsuspecting guests. Wade had been assigned to tail us at a distance and make the lights flicker as we walked throughout the inn, while Louise made the windows rattle with creepy music. Brian kept the temperature spookily low, and Jonathan lurked in the upstairs corridor and made creepy shadows appear on the walls to great effect.

Mart contributed by drifting along and occasionally slamming doors or turning off the lights, knowing that I wouldn't criticise him for once. I let him have his fun, and the tour went smoothly from start to finish. I had an easy time pretending not to see the ghosts in the background, and once we reached the lobby again, the ghosts gave us a round of applause so enthusiastic that all the downstairs doors and windows flew open.

"Oops," said Jia. "Better fix those."

As we dispersed throughout the inn, I glimpsed movement behind the automatic doors to the inn's lobby. When I approached, I found myself looking into Mr Cogman's glassy eyes.

"Please don't tell me you want to be part of the tour." *Didn't he vanish?* Had he somehow figured out how to hide himself in the afterworld? I peered closer at him and took a step back. "Guys, we have an intruder."

Mr Cogman's zombie, it seemed, had been revived from his frozen state at the morgue and walked all the way to the inn. And I bet he hadn't done so alone.

A scream rang out from the restaurant. *Carey.* Leaving Mr Cogman in the doorway, I ran towards the restaurant, where Tara's zombie lumbered towards Carey, blank-eyed and utterly insensible.

"Hey!" I shouted. "Get away from her."

Tara's reanimated body turned towards me, slowly. At least they weren't fast-moving—and were even slower now they'd been stuck in refrigerators for days—but why had someone sent them here?

Carey whimpered behind me, while I reached for the pulse of magic keeping Tara's body animated and gave a firm shove with my Reaper's touch. The zombie collapsed, and I heard Jia swearing at the top of her lungs from somewhere else in the inn.

If Tara and Mr Cogman were there, then Marilyn must be too. With Tara taken care of, I returned to the lobby and found Mr Cogman shuffling in the direction of the stairs.

"Don't you even think about it." I stepped in and dispatched him from behind, causing him to collapse into a heap.

Now to find the third zombie. Hearing another shout from Jia, I ran through into the restaurant again and tracked the noise down to the kitchen. Marilyn beat against the glass window atop the inn's back door, her face as blank as the other zombies'.

Jia popped up behind me, wielding a spatula. "Care to lend a hand?"

"With pleasure." I opened the door and shoved the zombie with both hands, shattering the spell that kept it standing. "I hope that's all of them."

I would not be thrilled if the killer's other victims' zombies were also wandering around town, but if their bodies had been stored elsewhere, they'd have a long way to walk. Still, the murderer had obviously sent them here for a reason.

Allie poked her head into the kitchen. "Another one?"

"The last one, I hope."

Jia and I carried Marilyn's body into the reception area and then went to fetch Tara's too. When we had all three of them in the lobby, under close watch, I called Drew.

"Hey," I said when he answered. "We just had a zombie attack at the inn. Do the staff at the morgue know their corpses got up and walked away?"

He swore. "I'll be right there."

"Bring enough people to carry all three bodies," I advised him. "I should probably supervise, too, in case the person who reanimated them is still hanging around."

That was what I got for thinking I'd get a night off, though I'd been too fixated on the police's arrest of the wrong person to wonder what had happened to the real killer's zombie-summoning habit.

Now I had zero doubt I'd been the target, but why? I could banish zombies in my sleep, though if the killer had been trying to freak out the others, they'd succeeded.

If I went with my theory that Mr White was to blame,

then it didn't quite add up. He must know I suspected him, since I hadn't exactly been subtle with my accusations, but all he'd needed to do was keep quiet and leave Simon behind bars, and the police would let him walk free. Sending the reanimated bodies of the victims to attack me was the opposite of subtle, and if he'd thought a few zombies would frighten me off, he was mistaken.

The police showed up within minutes, Drew leading the way in. The other officers picked up the bodies with a reluctance that was completely understandable, considering the corpses had been walking not long ago. Unfortunately, the female officer who'd taken issue with me going into Simon's house had come with them, and she seemed entirely too amused at my predicament.

"If I was the owner of this inn, then I'd be seriously reconsidering hiring someone who was such a magnet for zombies," she remarked.

I glared straight back. "Don't speak too soon. The night is young, and plenty of zombies might be waiting to ambush you too."

"That's enough, Petra," Drew said. "Perhaps Maura was targeted because she was close to finding the killer and therefore the biggest threat to exposing them."

"Exactly," I said. "Also, this is more proof that the man you have behind bars is innocent. Simon can't be the one who reanimated them."

"Can we take your word for it on that?" Petra queried. "I'm not familiar with spells for raising zombies, but if he raised them before he was arrested, then it doesn't matter."

"I broke the original reanimating spells myself, so this is new." I looked pointedly at the other officers. "Also, didn't you take his wand away from him when you locked him up?"

"Yes," Petra said, "but he might have an accomplice on the outside."

"I don't know if you're aware, but someone was hanging around the morgue yesterday who you were initially supposed to question at the time of Simon's arrest. Mr White. You might want to make questioning him a priority."

Come to think of it, if he'd sent the zombies, then he probably wasn't safe and snug in bed. He might even still be near the morgue, and if I moved fast enough, I might be able to catch him in the act. I couldn't use my Reaper abilities to track zombies, but I could certainly do so to the living.

"Mr White is still on our list for questioning," Drew said. "Petra, stop arguing with Maura and go and help the others with the bodies."

Petra obeyed, with reluctance, while I took in a breath and then called the shadows towards me.

"Maura, what are you doing?" asked Drew.

"I'm going to track Mr White," I told him in a low voice. "Using my Reaper powers. If I land on top of him and find him hiding in an alley or something, then I might be able to surprise a confession out of him."

He groaned. "Maura, I can't condone that. But I also can't stop you, so can you please try to avoid getting hurt?"

"Can't make any promises, but I can guarantee he won't see me coming."

I pictured Mr White firmly in my mind's eye as I leapt into the darkness. *Please don't let him be in the shower.*

I emerged from the darkness, crashing into a table in the middle of a crowded pub. Several people jumped to their feet, spilling pint glasses everywhere.

"It's the Reaper!" several voices exclaimed.

Beer drenched my limbs, while my knees throbbed from where I'd hit the table. Dazed and in pain, I finally spotted Mr White himself among the patrons, who looked nothing short of bewildered to see me there.

I might have scrambled for an excuse, but instead I legged it out of the pub before the patrons could demand I paid for the drinks I'd spilled.

Don't let anyone tell you I don't know how to throw a party.

———

The next morning dawned bright and angry. Or maybe that was just me. My knees were covered in bruises that rivalled the hit to my pride from the debacle I'd caused when I'd crashed into the pub, and for all that, it seemed Mr White hadn't raised the zombies after all.

Either that or he'd been quick to hide himself, which was entirely possible, but he'd picked the most crowded and conspicuous location in town.

I got out of bed and growled at Mart to get out of my shower so I could use it. I hadn't slept much, though it'd been late by the time I'd got back from accompanying the officers to the morgue. If any of them had wondered why I was limping, Drew's stern presence kept them from asking any questions. He'd gone into protective werewolf mode after I came hobbling back from the pub, and I wouldn't deny it was a turn-on. Pity he'd had to go back to work, leaving me to go to sleep alone. Or rather, lie awake expecting to be woken up by a call saying the bodies had got up and walked out of the morgue again. With the person who'd reanimated them still at large, that was only a matter of time.

Drew called me when I was on my way downstairs to breakfast.

"Hey," I answered. "Sorry about yesterday. I really thought I had him."

"Simon is going to be questioned today," he said. "I wondered if you'd like to talk to him first."

"Are you sure your fellow officers would like that?"

"Definitely not, but I'm the one calling the shots."

Relief flooded me, as did a wave of gratitude towards him. "Certain members of your team might do well to remember that I was the one who spared them from having to take the zombies to pieces with their own hands."

"I made that clear enough to them, don't worry," he said. "See you soon."

"I'll be there in fifteen minutes."

Mart declined to come with me in case the zombies made an appearance again, though last time they'd come to the inn itself, not the police station. Someone had been trying to send a message directly to me, but if it hadn't been Mr White, then who could it possibly have been?

The question remained lodged in my mind as I walked from the inn to the police station. Drew waited outside the brick building, looking as if he'd slept as little as I had. At least the kiss he planted on my lips woke me up slightly.

"Nice to see you too." I grinned at him and then

levelled a glare towards the police station. "Do the others seriously think Simon raised those zombies while he was behind bars?"

"He's going to have the chance to explain himself when we question him today," he said. "In the light of everything we found in his house, that's all we can give him."

"Except a chance to talk to the Reaper Witch. Just what you need when you're facing a lifetime jail sentence." I rolled my eyes. "Seriously, I feel like it's half my fault he's sitting in there."

"That is complete nonsense, Maura." He beckoned to me. "We should head in. I'll give you as much time with him as you need."

I could do little to make his situation worse, at the very least, but I followed Drew through the police station's lobby and into a long corridor where the holding cells were located. Simon sat on a bench in the nearest, and his eyes brightened when he saw me walk in. "Hello. Maura, is it?"

"Hey, there," I said. "Drew said I could come and talk to you before your trial."

His gaze dropped. "Right. I… I don't know what to say."

"I know you're innocent." I dropped my voice. "Someone planted that evidence in your cellar."

His expression clouded. "But who? I don't understand."

"I think I know who," I said. "You were an easy target, since you lived next door to Mr Cogman's house, but what I'd like to know is how they got into your house without being noticed. Are you sure you didn't hear anything?"

"It must have been while I was sleeping," he said. "And… I can only assume they used magic. A silencing spell, maybe, to mask the sound of their footsteps."

"We have a very dedicated serial killer," I agreed. "They also raised Mr Cogman and the two others' bodies from the morgue last night, did you hear?"

Simon's eyes widened. "Wait, was that what the officers were talking about earlier? I heard someone mention zombies…"

"You can't have done that from behind bars and without a wand," I said. "That's one point in your favour. Also, one of the victims' ghosts was around until recently, and her description of the place she died didn't match your cellar in the slightest."

"Will the police accept a ghost's word, though?"

"Unfortunately not," I said. "The physical evidence got in there somehow, and I think Mr White was the one who planted it there. Do you know him?"

"Ellis White?" He shook his head. "I wouldn't think… he seemed so polite whenever I saw him."

"You have seen him, then?"

"Once or twice," he murmured. "When he came to visit Mr Cogman… he seemed friendly enough."

"Were they really work colleagues?" I asked. "Because Mr Cogman was applying to work at the inn."

"Was he?" He frowned. "That's odd. I was sure he worked freelance. He had meetings with clients all the time."

"Did he?" Suspicion prickled up my spine. "How do you know? Did you talk to him?"

"I didn't ask him about work, but I often saw him

leaving the house for several days at a time. That was why I didn't realise he was missing at first."

Interesting. "Thanks for telling me."

"Of course. You're going to get me out of here, aren't you?"

"I'll do my best to."

I left the cells behind and found Drew waiting at the end of the corridor. "Did he have anything to say?"

"Only that he must have been asleep when the killer walked in and planted the evidence," I said. "And that Mr Cogman often took trips out of town for several days, supposedly for work-related reasons. I think you should ask Mr White more questions about their working relationship too."

"Assuming he's recovered from the fright you gave him yesterday."

I groaned. "It's not impossible that he hid in the nearest pub the instant he finished raising the zombies. I was too busy trying to avoid a dozen drunk blokes blaming me for spilling their drinks to question him last night."

With Mr Cogman's ghost gone, I had no evidence indicating Simon's innocence except that he couldn't raise zombies from a cell, and he couldn't prove he wasn't the one who'd killed them. The only thing that would set him free was proof of the actual killer.

"I'll keep you updated on Simon's trial," he told me. "What do you want to do now?"

"I think I'll drop by the morgue. I have a couple of questions I want to ask their team concerning how those zombies got out."

14

I walked directly from the police station to the morgue. I didn't hold out much hope that I'd get answers there, since the staff had avoided calling me even when they'd been autopsying former zombies, but I was out of ideas.

Outside the building, I made sure nobody was watching before tapping into my Reaper powers to search the afterworld. Nobody replied, but that I'd expected. Morgues weren't typical haunts for ghosts. According to Mart, they were creeped out at the idea of being near the dead, though he didn't speak for all ghosts. I'd worked at a morgue once. Less than a week passed before I'd grown so fed up with ghosts following me around asking me to pass on their funeral requests to their living relatives that I'd agreed to their wishes just so they would leave me alone. Shockingly, my employers hadn't been best pleased with me.

That was far from the first job I'd screwed up, and a Reaper Witch in the normal world had even fewer options than in the paranormal one. Now I'd finally found a corner of the paranormal world that accepted my level of weirdness, and I refused to let this serial killer ruin it all. We couldn't run ghost tours if random zombies might show up to freak out the guests, but Carey had put in too much effort for me to allow her dream to be ruined by a bunch of corpses.

I pushed open the door to the morgue and addressed the first person I saw, a guy who looked to be barely out of his teens. He attempted to hide behind a fridge when I walked in.

"Excuse me," I said pointedly.

The guy shuffled out, a sheepish look on his face. "Er, Maura, is it?"

"Yes. And you are?"

"Les." He twitched when I approached, his gaze darting towards the refrigerators. Worried another body would walk out of there, perhaps.

"I wanted to ask you a couple of questions about the incident last night," I told him. "To start off with, how did you not notice three of your bodies climb out of the fridge and wander out?"

His gaze dropped, a flush creeping across his face. "I… I went out for a smoke and heard a noise in here. When I came back in, the drawers were… they were trying to open by themselves. I panicked."

"Was anyone else in here?" I asked. "Like the person who reanimated them?"

He shook his head. "I didn't see anyone, but like I said, I backed off as soon as I saw the drawers shaking. I thought they might give up eventually, but they didn't, and then… then the three of them climbed straight out."

"And you let them walk out? Without calling the police?"

It wouldn't have made much of a difference if he had, but I didn't appreciate everyone acting as if I had nothing to offer as a Reaper until the last possible moment. As for the person who'd reanimated the zombies... they must have been close to the morgue at the time, but nobody had seen them.

"I tried to stop one of them from opening the drawer," he mumbled. "But he—he was too strong, and nothing would have stopped him."

"He didn't attack you?" I asked.

Another shake of the head. The person who brought them back must have told them not to harm anyone. Except me, maybe, but a zombie couldn't do much to a Reaper. No, the necromancer's main goal was to give me a warning, I was sure.

"May I look around?"

His shoulders slumped. "Sure, go ahead."

I circled the small, cold room, examining it from each angle. The zombies hadn't caused any obvious damage to the morgue, but how had the necromancer reached them in here? To have known which bodies to raise, the person responsible must have known exactly which drawers they'd been stored in... and Mr White had certainly been hanging around outside the morgue for long enough to find out. But I'd failed to catch him in the act, and thanks to the sage around the doors, no ghosts would have been close enough to observe the breakout either.

Speaking of which...

I came to a halt at the doorway. The sage was gone, and someone had broken the carefully arranged circle around the perimeter of the building. No wonder the zombies got out easily.

I spun on my heel. "Who removed the sage?"

"Huh?" said the teenage employee.

"The sage." I gestured. "It's gone."

Suspicions prickled at the back of my mind. I'd asked the staff to put sage around the entire building, since the alternative was risking Mr Cogman getting in and dragging his own body out of there by sheer force of will. If he hadn't disappeared, I'd blame it on him, but despite his strong ghostly presence, he'd been no match for whoever had made him disappear. After all, even the strongest ghost paled in comparison to the living. Pun intended. Yet Mr Cogman had vanished so suddenly that I'd forgotten our last encounter, in which he'd tried to get into the morgue and been furious to find sage blocking his way.

No one had any good reason to remove it, unless someone else who worked here hadn't realised why it was necessary. Or maybe it was one of the police officers who'd brought the bodies back yesterday. I should have checked, but I'd been exhausted, and it'd been dark outside besides.

The staff member wrinkled his nose. "Weird."

"Tell me about it."

What would be the point of removing the anti-ghost defences? Maybe it was a coincidence, but I had my doubts.

"Is anyone else in?" I asked the guy. "Staff, I mean?"

"Nah, it's just me. The boss is on a break."

"Right." No wonder they seemed so disorganised in here. "I need to find out who removed that sage from near the door, because it was why the zombies were able to get out. I'd also advise you to put more down in its place if you don't want any more undead intruders."

He blanched. "Okay. We have some in storage… We put it around the bodies while the autopsies were in progress."

That would explain why the zombies had stayed put—but not last night. "Good. Keep using it until I've caught the person pulling the strings."

Literally. The dead were nothing but pawns in this… except for Mr Cogman, whose death had been unlike any of the others and whose ghost had been a thorn in my side up until the moment of his disappearance.

"All right," said the employee. "Good luck."

"Cheers." I paused. "Also—did you see a guy hanging around outside the morgue last night? He was there a few times yesterday as well. Claimed to be a friend of Mr Cogman's."

His expression cleared. "Oh, I know who you mean."

"Did he come inside?"

"Yeah… he wanted to ask about the autopsy. Seemed nice enough."

I bet he did.

"Right. Thanks for telling me."

Leaving the morgue, I picked up on an odd herbal scent from nearby. A row of bushes bordered the cemetery, and the smell of sage drifted out. Had the person who'd removed the ghost-proof barrier from the doors dumped the herbs in here?

I crouched down and saw my guess confirmed. At least the pimply employee wouldn't have to beg the coven for supplies to douse the place in sage. After stashing the herbs in my pocket, I straightened upright, and the scent intensified.

A cloud of smoke rose to surround me, out of nowhere. Before I could blink, the world went black.

———

When I came back to consciousness, I found myself lying on my back, aching all over as if someone had thrown me down a hole. Which might well be true. The thick smell of herbs in the air didn't help my dizziness. It was too dark to see further than my own hand, and when I struggled into a sitting position, the ground was slightly damp. I reached back with my hands and felt the edges of a wall, confirming I was in a room. I didn't think it was a cave, but it was dark enough that I might be underground for all I knew.

Either way, I could theoretically use my Reaper abilities to get out, but that would mean forfeiting the chance to find out my location—and who exactly was responsible for my predicament.

"Hello?" My voice cracked, sounding like a rusty door. "Anyone there?"

"You know how difficult it is to find a way to capture a Reaper?"

Groggily, I looked up at the speaker and was completely unsurprised to recognise Mr White's voice.

"I'm shocked." I coughed. "Shocked that the guy who was hanging around the morgue and the house of one of the victims turned out to be the twisted serial killer."

"This isn't what you think," he said. "I really didn't want to harm you, Maura."

I struggled to drag my legs into a more comfortable position and failed. "Let me guess. You had to capture me because I got too close to guessing the truth? You weren't subtle, you know, with those zombies you sent to the inn."

"That wasn't me."

"Pull the other one." I sat back against the wall. "I suppose it wasn't you who set up this hideout of yours either. Could use better lighting, though."

A light snapped on, a single bulb hanging from the ceiling, revealing a narrow room that contained no furniture, nor any windows or doors. A stepladder at the back led up to a trapdoor, and in front of it, Mr Cogman's ghost appeared, drifting forward to join his living companion.

I stared at him for an instant. On one level, it didn't surprise me that his ghost had stuck around, given his stubbornness, but seeing him in person was another matter entirely. We couldn't be in Hawkwood Hollow anymore, so he'd obviously gone out of range of my Reaper powers... but had Mr White been lying when he'd claimed not to be able to see ghosts?

"Well done," I said. "Which of you is the murderer, and which raised the zombies from the dead? Or is it both of you?"

Either way, Mr Cogman must have been *really* mad at me to allow his own corpse to be raised from death and manipulated like a puppet. Right now, his expression consisted of a combination of his usual annoyance and an eerie calmness that gave me goose bumps. So did the dawning suspicion that I'd only scratched the surface of the plan these two had cooked up together. I could only assume Mr Cogman's own untimely death hadn't been a part of it, but other than that, he was an impressive actor as well as the obvious mastermind behind this scheme. All his ghostly temper tantrums were entirely for show.

"You don't seem to understand the predicament you are in," Mr Cogman said to me.

"Oh, I understand perfectly well," I said. "I should have sent you to the afterlife while I had the chance."

"You should have," he agreed.

"You killed all those people yourself," I said to Mr Cogman. "Or was it a joint effort? Work colleagues, huh. I see what you did there."

"You couldn't leave well enough alone."

"Who killed you, then?" I asked. "Was it true that someone jumped you on the street, or did you make that part up too?"

His eyes narrowed. "You still have no tact, do you?"

"Coming from a mass murderer." I addressed Mr White instead. "Go on, I can tell you're dying to tell me the full story. Was it you who told the police he was missing?"

"I had to," he said. "I had to make someone notice that he was murdered."

"By whom? One of his would-be victims?" I turned back to Mr Cogman. "You wanted my attention from the start, didn't you? Between pretending you wanted a job at the inn, to insisting I get involved in investigating your murder..."

"You were the one person who might have been able to stop me," he said. "I had to remove that possibility. If not by killing you, then by diverting your attention."

"Should I be flattered?" I said. "I'm guessing you had to rely on Mr White to do everything for you once you lost your corporeality. Must have been tricky when he can't see you."

"It was hard," Mr Cogman agreed. "But harder was dealing with your meddling. I thought that when you assumed me gone and the suspect arrested, you'd leave it alone."

"I suppose it was your idea to pin the murders on your neighbour."

"His relentless questions towards both of us came close to exposing the truth, so he was the natural choice," Mr Cogman confirmed. "He isn't nearly as pleasant as he seems."

Mr White lowered his gaze, looking faintly ashamed. "Someone had to take the fall."

"It should have been you." I could only assume he'd put up the obituary, too, just to ensure that Mr Cogman's death was discovered and the perpetrator arrested. "Why zombies, though? I get why you did it to Mr Cogman, because you wanted him to be discovered, but the others?"

"I didn't turn them into zombies," he said. "It was… an unintended side effect."

"Side effect." As my eyes adjusted to the light, I noticed the edges of the room. Chalk marks had been etched on the floor, while herbs were scattered around the edges of a circle. Not sage either. "This is your ritual, then. What were you trying to do? Sacrificing that many people just to turn them into zombies never made any sense to me."

"It wasn't my intention to turn anyone into zombies," Mr Cogman growled. "I did it to my own body because it was the only way to get it back home to Hawkwood Hollow, but the unstable energy in this room means that any bodies left in here often rise of their own accord. Since the last two victims were still in this room when I was killed, before I could dispose of their bodies…"

Disgust rose within me. "They rose from death, so you sent them back home. I suppose you hoped the zombie spell would wear off before anyone discovered them."

"That's usually how it ends," he confirmed, "but this is an unusually powerful ritual. There was a reason I set it up outside of Hawkwood Hollow, aside from the obvious benefits of a lower risk of discovery."

"Yes, very clever of you." I couldn't believe I was even having a sane conversation with a twisted serial killer. "Care to tell me what you planned to use the ritual *for*?"

"None of your concern," he said. "It *did* mean that death was merely a setback to me. After all, there's enough energy in this room to allow my spirit to possess a new body."

"A new body." The truth hit me. That was the real reason he'd brought me here without killing me outright. "That's not going to work out in your favour."

"Why not?"

"Because I'm a Reaper. I'm pretty sure we're immune to ghosts possessing our bodies. It goes with the territory."

Ghosts were rarely strong enough to possess a person's body on their own, but it *was* possible to bind a spirit to the body of another person by using the exact kind of creepy ritual magic that Mr Cogman had been dabbling in already. Each life sacrificed generated energy, an invisible force like that which kept zombies walking past their deaths, and the room was thrumming with it.

But would the ritual work on a Reaper? I didn't know

for sure, because I'd never heard of anyone being foolish enough to try.

"You're lying," Mr Cogman said. "Vampires are immune to possession, yes, but a half Reaper like you should be simple to handle. There's more than enough energy in this room to dislodge your soul from your body and put mine in its place."

Dislodge. Lovely term. It seemed too innocuous for the subject of ripping out someone's soul. Namely, mine.

"It won't be as easy as all that, I guarantee it." Being a Reaper wasn't genetically inherited like being a witch or werewolf, but our magic was given to us through a special kind of training open to very few people. In fact, it was common for the Reaper Council to take the ability away entirely from anyone who left their ranks. They hadn't done so with me, though... so if his plan worked, then he'd have full access to my Reaper powers.

I couldn't let that happen. I had to get out of here first.

How long had I been unconscious? Did Drew know I was gone? Allie would certainly have noticed I hadn't come back to the inn, but she'd probably concluded that I'd gone to help Drew with the case, and she wouldn't raise the alarm. That dopey employee at the morgue probably hadn't even seen Mr White ambush me outside, while the police never had found the location where the original victims were killed. I was on my own.

Mr Cogman's mouth twisted in a grin. "At least this time I won't have to deal with disposing of the body."

"Lovely. I suppose you buried the others?"

"I did but not so thoroughly that I couldn't dig them up again. Like I said, they tend to rise of their own accord when they're around this level of magical energy… so I helped them along a little. Or Ellis did, anyway."

A chill rose to my arms. "You had Mr White wake up all the zombies?"

Mr White gave me a sideways look, not hearing the other side of the conversation, and said, "They won't harm anyone."

Mr Cogman gave a humourless smile. "But they *will* ensure your friends are too busy to rescue you."

He'd sent them to Hawkwood Hollow. A whole swarm of zombies. I rose upright, but a wave of dizziness pushed me down. The effects of the spell Mr White used to subdue me hadn't faded yet, and other spells were at work in this room, chalked onto the walls and floor and ceiling. Trapping me in here.

Ready to tear out my soul and let Mr Cogman's take its place.

"You know, I'm really not that keen on the idea of giving up my body."

Doing my best to ignore the dizziness, I called the shadows to my hands. Barely a flicker of darkness stirred. He'd short-circuited my Reaper abilities, which I should have seen coming. I'd bet he'd used a similar method to the one the coven had when they'd booby-trapped their office, yet for all my suspicions, they hadn't been involved after all. Mr Cogman was the true mastermind, with Mr White as his accomplice—and his hands and voice.

Mr White faced the circle marked on the floor and held up a piece of paper in his hands, speaking words under his breath I couldn't hear or understand.

Okay, that's enough of that.

I reached into my pocket, hoping that he'd forgotten to

take my wand, but no such luck. Instead, I found something even better: the sage I'd pocketed after finding it in the bushes outside of the morgue.

I watched Mr Cogman's ghost for a moment. He supervised the ritual without saying a word or looking at me. He might be strong, but he was still a ghost. He was relying on Mr White to act as his proxy, to do the actual magic, and he didn't think for a second that I might target him instead.

At least until I threw the sage into his face.

15

M r Cogman recoiled with a howl of indignation, stopping Mr White's recitation as he realised I'd attacked his ghostly friend. The sage didn't touch Mr Cogman physically, but it had the same effect on him as it would on any spirit, and when I flung a second handful at him, his ghost flew straight through the wall and out of the room altogether.

"Stop that!" Mr White protested.

I grinned. "Handy to have a little ghost-repellent with you at all times, isn't it? I'm guessing he'll find it tricky to possess my body when he isn't in the room."

I began sprinkling a line of sage on top of the chalk marks, but Mr White reached forward and grabbed my arm. "Give that here."

I let him pull me forward, out of the circle. Then I rammed my elbow into his nose. He released me with a choked noise of pain, and I kicked him in the kneecap for good measure. The lightbulb shone on my wand, which he'd discarded on the floor and which I grabbed in one hand before making my escape.

The stepladder led me into a narrow hallway that contained several doors. The only one that interested me was the cracked wooden door that led outside.

"You like burying things in cellars, don't you?" I called to Mr Cogman. "I have to admit the cuddly teddy bear collection was a nice touch to your cover story."

No response came from the ghost. He must have fled outside, so I crossed to the front door and shouldered it open. As it turned out, the killer's hideout wasn't in a field but at the bottom of what looked like a ditch.

"This house was buried in the accident that followed the flooding of the river," said Mr White from behind me. He spoke thickly, his nose bleeding from where I'd hit him. "Nobody ever came back to fix the damage."

"The ideal hideout for a serial killer, huh." Where had Mr Cogman's ghost disappeared to? I couldn't see him, but a ghost would have a far easier time climbing the muddy trench than I would.

Mr White reached out to grab me from behind, but I dodged and stuck out a foot, tripping him up. Outside the house, I slammed the door in his face and then studied the area in an attempt to get my bearings. The house appeared to be half-buried underneath a hill, which explained why nobody had found it yet. I saw the river nearby as a darkened ribbon twisting into the distance, which meant Hawkwood Hollow must be within walking distance.

It was no wonder the ghosts hadn't been able to find their way back, though—assuming Mr Cogman hadn't banished them right away, which he might have. His ability to see ghosts had played in his favour even before he'd become one of them.

Mr White hurried up the hill behind me. "I meant that I never wanted to hurt you, Maura, but—"

"But you're committed to helping your mass-murderer friend," I finished. "He seems to have done a runner. Or whatever the ghostly equivalent is."

He pointed his wand at me, and I fought the urge to sigh. I didn't know if my Reaper abilities were still cut off, but I pulled out my wand and continued to back up the hill, not taking my eyes off him.

"I wish you wouldn't make this difficult, Maura," he said. "You should know, I'm not as accomplished a wizard as Alan is, but I'm more than a match for you, especially with your Reaper abilities no longer functioning."

That answered that question, then. Undeterred, I pointed my wand at the ground below his feet. "I'm sure you are, but I'm tired of listening to you."

With one flick of my wand, the sloping hill collapsed beneath his feet, thick mud rising to his knees and then his waist. I flicked my wand again and sent his wand spinning from his hand, out of reach, while he struggled and flailed.

Looking up at me, he flinched. "Please don't kill me."

"I'm not like you, Mr White." I backed further up the hill, conscious of the unsteady ground beneath my own feet. "I'm not a cold-blooded killer. You might pretend to have a conscience and regrets, but whatever that ritual was, it couldn't have been worth sacrificing lives for."

"There's a bigger picture to this," he said. "Magic has more potential than the covens and those who run the magical world want us to know. Take rituals, for instance."

"It looks to me like you're killing people to use their life force for your own purposes." Most necromantic rituals were banned for that fundamental reason. Even summoning a ghost required a sacrifice of sorts, if you counted throwing herbs and plants into the spell as a sacrifice, but it wasn't the same as sacrificing *people.*

"*I* don't," he said. "Alan was the visionary of the pair of us."

"What did you do, bring him the victims?" I guessed. "That makes you an accomplice, and I'm more than happy to ensure you'll spend the rest of your life on the inside of a cell if you ever get out of that hole."

I didn't wait to hear his reply. I didn't even care who'd killed Mr Cogman anymore. Really, they'd done us all a favour by exposing his crimes. Even if they'd also inadvertently forced him to readapt his ritual and divert his efforts towards getting himself a new body—specifically, mine. I shuddered all over with revulsion at the very thought, gladly turning my back on the house and walking uphill until I'd left the killer's lair in the dust.

Mr White wasn't in any danger of following me now that I'd buried him up to his neck in the dirt. A fitting end, though not a permanent one. I'd need to come back to retrieve him later... once I found Mr Cogman. Not to mention his zombies.

I aimed my path for the river and scanned the banks for Hawkwood Hollow, spying a cluster of houses on the other side of a mass of fields. I didn't see any zombies yet, but Mr Cogman didn't seem the type to make idle threats.

I followed the path of the river for a while, cursing Mr

White for cutting off my Reaper abilities when I could really have used the power to jump through the shadows. As it was, I had to go on foot while dizzy and aching from my kidnapping attempt, hoping that I'd find a witch or wizard to undo the spell on me. Jia would, of course, but the inn was a long way from here. From the angle, I'd ended up on the opposite side of town. Typical.

As for the coven? While Mina Devlin might have approved of ritual murders, this wasn't the coven's work. Not the current one, anyway, though it wouldn't surprise me if she'd known about Mr Cogman, given their shared interests. Ugh.

When I reached the outskirts of Hawkwood Hollow, I finally stumbled across the zombies. It wasn't hard to spot a group of ten or so people staggering through the street at a jerky pace, not interacting with one another, and I didn't have to run to catch up to them from behind.

As I neared the first zombie, I tried to sense the thread of life keeping them walking but failed. I needed to get my power back before I could get rid of them.

Darting down a side street, I overtook the zombies and made my way towards the centre of town. Once I reached the high street, I aimed for the police station and marched straight through the automatic doors. Drew, who'd been talking to another officer in the entryway, stopped to stare at me. "Maura. What—?"

"Zombies," I gasped out. "They're coming—Mr White sent them, but Mr Cogman is here. It was him all along."

"Mr Cogman?" He strode to my side, taking in my dishevelled appearance with wide eyes. "I thought his ghost disappeared."

"He was hiding out in the middle of nowhere—at the

killer's house." I sucked in a breath. Man, I was exhausted. "I subdued Mr White and left him ready for the police to pick up, but he and Mr Cogman sent the zombies of all his other victims to come here to keep everyone too distracted to come looking for me. I can't get rid of them until I get someone to reverse this spell on me."

"What spell?"

"Mr White blocked my Reaper powers. Without them, I can only get rid of those zombies the hard way, and I don't think anyone wants that."

"No, I can't imagine they do," he said. "Where did you say Mr Cogman was?"

"I think he's on his way to the inn." He was still furious with me, after all, and while he might be a ghost, he was a powerful one and not to be underestimated. Given what he'd done to the other ghosts, he was also as dangerous to the dead as the living.

He swore. "I'll send my officers after the zombies. The ghost…"

"I'll deal with him myself."

I'd wasted too much time already, but I'd have zero hope of getting rid of the zombies *or* Mr Cogman if I didn't have my Reaper powers. After leaving the police station, I went to the first place I had hope of finding a witch or wizard with the skill to help me. Namely, the coven's headquarters.

When I came bursting through the front doors, several witches in the lobby stopped to gawp at me.

"You!" Wendy's eyes bulged. "What are you doing here in such a frightful state?"

"There's a group of zombies marching towards town," I told the staring witches. "The police would appreciate your help with subduing them before they cause too much panic."

Leaving them to think on that one, I aimed for the stairs. Wendy ran after me, wringing her hands. "Where are you going? You can't see the boss like that."

"I need to ask her a favour," I said over my shoulder.

At the top of the stairs, I made for Jennifer Ness's office. Without waiting for an invitation, I knocked once and then pushed the door inward.

Jennifer rose to her feet upon seeing my mud-stained clothes and obvious breathlessness. "What are you doing here? You're filthy."

"I was held hostage by a serial killer," I told her. "I need someone to undo the spell blocking my Reaper powers so I can get rid of the zombies that are currently on their way to Hawkwood Hollow."

"Someone to do *what?*" she said. "Are you asking me to do you a favour?"

"I'd appreciate it, considering the only other way to get rid of those zombies is a lot messier and might involve living people getting hurt," I said. "Also, the serial killer's mad ghost is loose in town somewhere as well, and only I can get rid of him."

Her eyes narrowed. "Anyone else might have helped you. You came to me specifically on purpose, didn't you?"

"Yes, I did," I said. "I wanted to see whose side you were really on."

"I am on nobody's side but my own." She pulled out her wand and pointed it at me. Hoping I hadn't made the wrong call, I held still and waited for her to cast the spell.

With a wave of her wand, the shadows returned to my

hands, and some of the dizziness faded. That was an improvement.

"Thanks," I said. "Zombies move slowly, so with luck, I'll be back before they reach the high street."

"Back from where?"

"The inn." I'd deal with the zombies only after I was certain that Carey and the others were safe.

Leaving her office, I ran back downstairs, brushing off every witch who tried to ambush me. From the high street, I made for the bridge over the river, after which I slowed my pace and approached the inn warily, keeping both eyes open for any signs of Mr Cogman. None appeared, but the guy was sneaky enough to hide in plain view. I didn't trust him an inch.

When I reached the inn's front doors, I found them wedged shut. My fears were confirmed: he'd taken the others hostage inside the inn itself.

"Let them out," I warned.

No response came from Mr Cogman. Instead of forcing the doors open, I stepped into the shadows and emerged inside the lobby itself. As the darkness faded, I spotted Carey and Allie standing on the other side of the automatic doors connecting the reception area to the restaurant. Their arms were around one another, faces horror-stricken, while the lights flickered overhead. Jia stood nearby, too, though she looked more annoyed than scared. When I drew closer, I spied her wand—and the others'—drifting up on the ceiling, out of her reach. She had no way to fight back. Mr Cogman, it seemed, had decided to start a ghost tour of his own.

"Mr Cogman," I called out. "I'm here. Let's finish this."

Shadows surrounded my hands just as Mr Cogman

appeared in front of me, his expression back to its usual scowl. "This wasn't necessary, you know. If you'd stayed put, I would have left them alone."

"And let you possess me? No thanks." I glared back at him. "For the record, I left Mr White buried alive back there. Was he really the best accomplice you could have picked?"

"He doesn't ask annoying questions."

"No, he brings you victims to sacrifice, doesn't he?" I queried. "How many have you killed? To what end?"

"It doesn't matter now," he said. "Thanks to that meddling witch, Tara."

"It was her who bumped you off, then?" Wait—hadn't she already been dead at the time? "How'd she do it?"

"She was strong, for a ghost. They all are. It's why I usually get rid of them."

"But you failed with her." A satisfied smile came onto my face. "That had to sting a little, didn't it? To be brought down by one of the very ghosts you tried to sacrifice."

Anger flickered through his gaze. "She undid all my work. Reduced me to this state."

"My heart bleeds for you," I said. "For the record, I'm not all that keen on letting your army of zombies overrun the town either, so we'd better get this over with."

"Hardly an army," he said. "It had to be done, Maura. You forced my hand."

A scream came from the adjoining room, and the lights flickered. *Carey.* He hadn't hurt the others—yet—but that didn't mean he would refrain from harming them if he thought it would anger me.

This had gone on too long already. I had to stop this.

I lunged at him, shadows at my fingertips, but he

glided out of reach. He might be solid for a ghost, but keeping hold of him was like trying to keep hold of a piece of soap, and he slipped through my grasp every time I came close to snagging him.

Then in a blink, he vanished and reappeared on the other side of the restaurant door. Carey screamed again when he grabbed her from behind.

Enough.

Shadows spread from my feet, covering the area around me, and I shouted his name with all the Reaper power I possessed. *"Alan Cogman!"*

Even a ghost as strong as he couldn't resist the call of a Reaper. His ghost popped up in front of me, indignant and incensed. He spun on his heel and tried to float away, but the shadows covered every possible route of escape. At my command, they spread, covering the entire reception area until nothing was visible but the darkness—and the outline of a door etched in light.

The door to the true afterlife, which beckoned him into the next world.

"I will not leave," he snarled. "I won't."

I'd figured he'd need some encouragement, which I was more than happy to provide. I grabbed his wrists and wrestled him towards the door, but I hadn't moved far before a bolt of energy zapped my hands like an electric shock, forcing me to let go.

"Ow," I ground out. "You took in the power from the ritual after all, didn't you?"

He floated before me with a self-satisfied expression. "Yes, and I can still take your body—by force."

"I don't think so." I lunged at him, but a blast of cold air hit me, pushing me back. He raised his palms, which crackled with power. He'd learned to harness the after-world against me, which proved that I'd definitely let him stick around for too long.

Powerful or not, though, he was dead, and I was a Reaper. Instead of reaching for him, I grabbed the door to the afterworld with one hand and shoved it open. Light spilled through the shadows, too bright to look at.

With my other hand, I seized his arm, ignoring the painful shock the thrumming energy sent through my limbs. Then I gave him a firm shove in the direction of the door. "Go, move on, and quit bugging me."

Mr Cogman's ghost flailed at the edge of the door, mouth open in indignation, but even he couldn't fight the call of the next world. When I released him, the light beyond the door drew him into its embrace.

"Goodbye, and good riddance, Mr Cogman." The door vanished along with the shadows, and I lowered my hands, my body trembling with the aftershocks. Exhaustion pressed heavily upon my shoulders.

The door slid open, and Carey, Allie, and Jia came running into the lobby.

"Is it over?" Carey asked.

I inclined my head. "Yeah. He's gone."

Sending him onward should have also broken his hold on the zombies, though someone would have to collect all the bodies. I didn't envy them that task, but at least their families would have closure. The police needed to fetch Mr White from his muddy prison, too, and clean up the mess the zombies had left behind.

I, however, intended to have a very long, hot shower, followed by an equally long nap. I'd earned that much.

16

Our first ghostly movie night started with the *My Little Pony* movie, as chosen by Vicky. I'd kept my word to her, and surprisingly Mart hadn't kicked up a fuss, though I'd had to negotiate to let him watch *Star Wars: A New Hope* next. While the ghosts crowded around the TV in the games room, I sought out Carey near the door.

"This'll get them motivated to start their first tour," I whispered to her. "Do you have any bookings yet?"

"My mum told me there's been a few later in the month," she said. "More will come as the word gets out, I think. It's been a great boost to my blog, getting all those viewers."

"Good."

As well as filming the test run of our actual ghost tour —minus the aftermath with the zombies—she'd also kept the camera rolling throughout her ordeal yesterday when she and the others were trapped in the inn at Mr

Cogman's hands. It'd taken the better part of the week for her to edit the footage to make the ghostly interference look intentional and not like the result of a spirit who genuinely wanted to cause harm. Since the camera hadn't shown the ghost himself, though, she'd managed to pull it off and upload it to her blog.

Once we had the footage sorted out, Carey had also uploaded it on several sites on the Wizarding Web specifically for advertising haunted hotels and inns, and interest didn't take long to trickle in. It helped that our ghosts were genuine, while a fair proportion of the advertised properties were fakes. Others did have genuine ghosts but ones who couldn't do much more than make curtains flutter or who refused to obey their human hosts.

"I got a dozen comments on the first day asking when we were going to open up tours," she said. "I had to tell everyone to wait until we were ready, so I hope they all come back."

"We did have to wait to make sure there definitely weren't any zombies left on the streets first," I reminded her. "That would have put off our guests."

"True."

The cleanup process had taken a while, though as I'd predicted, the zombies had all collapsed the instant I'd banished Mr Cogman's ghost to the true afterworld. Someone had needed to pick them all up, and there'd been an understandable shortage of volunteers. Jennifer Ness had not elected to help. Undoing the spell on me had been her sole act of generosity, and I'd been lucky to get that much.

Behind Carey, the door opened, and Allie entered the games room. "Maura, Drew's here."

"Oh, good."

Drew and I had seen each other a couple of times since the events of the past week, but I'd mostly been there to supervise his officers when they returned the former zombies to their homes. The atmosphere was not exactly date-like, but he'd claimed my presence would reassure the officers that none of the bodies would wake up and wander off. It didn't seem to matter how many times I told them that the guy responsible for reanimating them now resided in the permanent afterlife.

The one upside was that they'd stopped reprimanding me for supposedly interfering with their ability to do their jobs. It didn't hurt that I was the one who'd found the hideout they'd been searching for all week—by getting kidnapped, admittedly, but still.

I left the games room and met Drew in the reception area, where he greeted me with a kiss that made me severely regret that we didn't have a scheduled movie night of our own, just for the two of us.

"I didn't interrupt anything important, did I?" He indicated the closed door and the music drifting from inside the games room.

"Nah, the ghosts wanted to watch a movie."

"You mean your new staff members?"

"Yeah, we're rewarding them with movie nights. Since we can't pay them in cash, it's a compromise that worked out pretty well for everyone."

"Good idea," he replied. "What are they watching? A cartoon?"

"*My Little Pony*. Vicky's idea. She's just a kid."

He grinned. "I bet your brother isn't happy."

"We're watching *Star Wars* next, so he's being surprisingly tolerant," I said. "After Mr Cogman, I can wrangle those ghosts with my eyes closed."

"Does that mean you're free for a date night?"

"Only if it's here." I'd mostly recovered from my ordeal, but my lingering tiredness had returned with a vengeance after a day working behind the bar. "I know it's probably boring to keep eating at the same place, but if you want to go elsewhere in town, I'm using my Reaper powers to get there, not my feet."

"I like it here, so I'm not bothered." He beckoned me to follow him into the restaurant. "Unless it's a scheme to convince me to watch cartoons with your ghostly employees."

"Would you say yes if I asked you?"

"If *you* asked me?" He tilted his head. "I'd consider it. We haven't spent nearly enough time together lately."

"And entirely too much of it dealing with zombies, I know."

We entered the restaurant, where Jia had taken over the bar for the evening so that one of us would be free to kick off the ghostly movie night. She waved at me, and I waved back. I'd had to talk her out of taking over every one of my shifts after my return from my impromptu kidnapping, given that I hadn't suffered any permanent injuries other than a hit to my pride. Getting knocked out cold by a worm like Mr White was bound to humble me, but I had energy enough left for a date night with Drew. With luck, the movie would keep the other ghosts distracted for long enough to stay out of trouble.

Drew and I ordered our meals and caught up on everything we hadn't had time to discuss over the past few days. Namely, our rapid stride towards making

Hawkwood Hollow's ghostly inhabitants into a tourist attraction.

"When are you starting the tours?" he asked.

"Less than two weeks from now," I replied. "We've had a lot of interest, if you can believe it."

"I do believe it. Carey did a good job with the ads."

"She did. She's a natural entrepreneur." And good with people, which was more than I could say for myself. I was still working on earning the other ghosts' trust, though Mr Cogman's absence had been a considerable boost to everyone's morale. "I'd rather keep the zombies to a minimum, though."

"Most sane people would agree with you," he said. "My officers are going to be jumpy around dead bodies for a while."

"Better that they are, rather than complacent," I said. "Whatever Mr Cogman was doing with that ritual might have had knock-on effects I'm not even aware of yet."

"Come again?" he said. "Nobody on my staff can explain what the ritual was for, including the witches and wizards."

"There's a reason ritual magic is banned," I clarified. "Aside from the fact that most people who use it tend to have a loose relationship with morals, that is."

"Because they usually kill people in the process?" he queried. "I get that part. I'm just lost on this… energy stuff." He waved a hand vaguely. "It comes across as wishy-washy to me."

"That's because you're a shifter. You're more practical, focused on the here and now. It's probably why you can't see ghosts."

"I have no complaints on that front. Just seeing what you have to deal with is enough to put me off for life."

"I don't really have a choice in the matter," I said. "Anyway, about the 'energy stuff', as you call it, that's what ghosts are. Energy. Souls. A powerful ritual requires an equally strong source of energy to fuel it."

"To achieve what, though?"

"Well, Mr Cogman's end goal was to generate enough energy to rip out my soul and then possess my body." I pulled a face. "As for his original goal… most witches and wizards with an interest in rituals tend to want to amass power. Or summon things from the afterworld. Nasty things."

"Like those hellbeasts?"

"Don't remind me." I shuddered at the memory. "Anyway, the zombies were a result of the energy from the ritual going haywire and essentially reanimating any bodies within range. That hideout of Mr Cogman's was brimming with power that had nowhere to go."

His brow arched. "What happened to it after you left, then?"

"The energy will have dissipated," I said, though I wasn't completely sure. "Or the local farmers will have an unpleasant zombie problem for a few days."

"I hope not," he said. "The initial aim wasn't to raise zombies, though, right?"

"No, but Mr Cogman's original ritual got derailed by him ending up dead."

"Because the ghost of one of his victims killed him," he said. "Do you have any idea how hard this is going to be to explain in our police reports?"

"I have some idea, given past experience."

He gave me a half smile. "I suppose you do. And it's hard for my officers to deny that Simon was innocent. He's free to go."

"I'm glad." Simon's imprisonment had been unfair from the start, but I didn't fault the officers for believing the physical evidence was proof enough without anything else to go on. After the kidnapping incident, they'd wasted no time in hauling Mr White to jail after the officers had dug him out of the hole that I'd buried him in.

As for the house, I'd advised them to burn it to the ground so no one else could go in there and try to complete the ritual. I hoped that would be enough to quell whatever malevolent energy Mr Cogman had tapped into.

"Same here," Drew said. "Mr White is facing a lifetime behind bars. Mr Cogman deserves the same, but you delivered an appropriate fate upon him."

"By shoving him into the next world," I agreed. "He put up a hell of a fight, but I got rid of him in the end."

"You should really get compensation for what you do, Maura," he said. "Honestly."

"Reapers don't get paid."

His brows shot up. "Hang on… they don't? What's the incentive, then?"

"Someone has to do it," I said. "Reapers don't *need* things. Except a roof over their heads, and even that's a luxury. True Reapers don't need to eat, drink, or sleep, so it's optional. Us half-Reapers have it rough."

"No wonder you walked away."

"Yeah, but I'm no witch either." I grimaced. "I suppose I can strike the coven off my suspect list for ghost-related nonsense for a while, at least. Jennifer did help me."

"Eventually," he said. "I'm still not a fan of how she got

herself instated as leader without informing me. I'll be keeping an eye on that one."

"Wise idea. One of us has to." I stifled a yawn with the back of my hand.

"You're tired," he said. "You're not still working at the bar even after what you went through?"

"Why is everyone acting as if I'm on my deathbed?"

"You almost were," he reminded me. "Mr Cogman intended to… to possess you?"

"It wouldn't have worked," I told him. "To possess someone, you have to force their soul out of *their* body first, and Reapers are tough."

"Still." His mouth turned down at the corners, and he took my hand across the table. "I prefer your body when you're the one inside it."

"Was that supposed to be a come-on?"

"If you want to interpret it in that way. I have the rest of the night free."

My skin tingled, my body now very much wide awake. "I take it you don't want to join the ghosts' movie night?"

"If that's what you want to do, I can suffer through it," he said. "But I have more interesting things in mind."

So did I. I let him pull me to my feet, and Jia shot me a wink from behind the bar. Taking that to mean she'd keep Mart distracted for a while if he got bored with the movie, I walked hand in hand with Drew back to the inn.

We wouldn't have much time to ourselves after tonight. After all, it wouldn't be long before the inn became busy with its ghost tour schedule, and I had no illusions that everything would run completely smoothly from the get-go.

This night, though? It was ours, and it would definitely be zombie-free. I'd make sure of it myself.

ABOUT THE AUTHOR

Elle Adams lives in the middle of England, where she spends most of her time reading an ever-growing mountain of books, planning her next adventure, or writing. Elle's books are humorous mysteries with a paranormal twist, packed with magical mayhem.

She also writes urban and contemporary fantasy novels as Emma L. Adams.

Visit http://www.elleadamsauthor.com/ to find out more about Elle's books.